Buckingham Pet Palace is known for treating dogs like royalty—until murder dethrones its good reputation!

As owner of an upscale doggy daycare and spa, animal-lover Sue Patrick pampers pooches for the most elite clients in Lewes, Delaware. Surely she can survive a weeklong visit from Lady Anthea Fitzwalter, her well-to-do business partner from England. But before Sue can serve her guest a spot of tea, she discovers more-than-a-spot of blood inside the company van—and all over the driver's dead body . . .

Someone abandoned the van full of dogs at the Lewes ferry terminal and got away with murder, leaving Sue and Lady Anthea pawing for clues. With a fundraising gala approaching and Buckingham Pet Palace facing scandal, can two very different women work together to fetch the culprit from a list of dodgy suspects—or are they heading toward a proper disaster?

Visit us at www.kensingtonbooks.com

Books by Lane Stone

Pet Palace Mysteries
Stay Calm and Collie On

Published by Kensington Publishing Corporation

Stay Calm and Collie On

A Pet Palace Mystery

Lane Stone

LYRICAL PRESS
Kensington Publishing Corp.
www.kensingtonbooks.com

First Electronic Edition: November 2017
eISBN-13: 978-1-5161-0190-0
eISBN-10: 1-5161-0190-1

First Print Edition: November 2017
ISBN-13: 978-1-5161-0191-7
ISBN-10: 1-5161-0191-X

Printed in the United States of America

This book is dedicated to the Delaware River and Bay Lighthouse Foundation board members for all you do to preserve the Harbor of Refuge Lighthouse for future generations.

Chapter 1

"Sue! Hi!" My customer gave the Buckingham Pet Palace lobby a furtive once-over. "Is *she* here?"

No need to say who *she* was.

I propped my elbows on the reception counter and lowered my voice like I was about to reveal news to her and her alone, secrets people would kill for. "Her flight from Heathrow landed on time. She flew into Dulles. The driver called me from there and then again when they crossed the Bay Bridge." I was happy to indulge her curiosity with minute details; after all, I had worked long and hard to get everyone in Lewes, Delaware talking about Lady Anthea Fitzwalter. The whole town seemed to be looking forward to the first visit of our very own royal personage.

"Good afternoon, Lydia." My head groomer, Mason, joined us, leading a geriatric beagle. He handed our customer the leash, then pivoted to give me a tired, put-upon nod.

"Thanks for fitting us in. I wanted Loopy to look his best for Friday's gala." Mason turned back to her and managed a weak smile. I telepathically dared him to point out that the beagle looked pretty much the same after a groom as before, the exception being the Union Jack bandana Loopy now wore. Though only in his mid-twenties, Mason was one of the best dog groomers in Delaware. This particular dog had hardly been a challenge, still I complimented him on a job well done. But received no acknowledgment.

"You look tired," she cooed. Bingo! That's what Mason was longing to hear.

"Exhausted. You have no idea." Mason reached a toned and heavily tattooed arm down to give Loopy one final behind-the-ear scratch, then dragged himself away, calling over his shoulder, "I did teeth and glands."

She turned back to me. "Sue, is he okay?"

"He's loving every minute of it." Mason's hangdog expression hadn't fooled me at all. He tells me weekly that he's an artist. On Saturday he told me he was suffering for his art. I slid Lydia's credit card slip across the counter and showed her where to sign. "Both of my groomers are booked solid getting all the dogs ready for the gala." Abby, my standard Schnauzer, still needed to be groomed. It was only Monday, so I wasn't worried. I discreetly tucked the receipt into a cellophane bag along with a gluten-free dog treat in the shape of a blow-dryer.

She patted her shoulder bag. "I have my invitation right here. Engraved, even. Oh, my. Very nice." She paused in her quick sentences. "Might we see Lady Fitzwalter during the week here?"

"Oh, yes. She'll be in and out all week. Drop by anytime for tea." I pointed to the table of Twinings tea and Wedgwood mugs, which we have out every day. Our usual fare of Walkers shortbread had been replaced by the more labor-intensive clotted cream and scones. Of course, the Savannah Road Bake Shop had done the heavy lifting in baking the pastries. I'd purchased the clotted cream from a British specialty grocer in Wilmington. Though Walkers sported the coat of arms and the words, *By Appointment HM the Queen*, showing their Royal Warrant status, I wanted something special for my co-owner's visit.

Our contract allowed Buckingham Pet Palace to use her likeness and her name, but Lady Anthea had gone above and beyond that with her frequent emails, sometimes asking astute business questions, sometimes attaching photos for me to use. I appreciated all she'd done to make the Pet Palace a success and I wanted her to know it.

The front door opened and my afternoon receptionist floated in. Dana would be starting her senior year at Cape Henlopen High School next month. She has the biggest afro in the history of the world. My blond hair is cut short, so balance was maintained in the hair universe.

"Hi, Dana," Lydia and I said at the same time.

"Hey!" She and her hair leaned over to pet Loopy. She's truly beautiful— not pretty, not attractive—but beautiful. She takes advantage of our relative proximity to Manhattan to model part-time. I wondered how many hours she would be able to work at Buckingham's in the fall and how much time she'd spend in New York, beefing up her college fund.

Loopy lay down and rolled over on his back. A blatant appeal for a belly rub from Dana. Lydia shook her head. "None of that, young man. They have a party to put on," she said, giving the leash a slight tug. The dog reluctantly accepted defeat and stood. "See you Friday," she called on their way out.

"Bye. Don't forget to come back any afternoon for tea," I called.
Then I turned to Dana. "Am I ever glad to see you! It's been crazy here."
She came around to join me behind the desk. "And it's only Monday."
She looked at the dashboard document on the computer screen. "Looks like
we have double the number of dogs in day camp than usual!" She checked
to be sure the lobby was empty, then she broke into a little dance. "Yayus!"

I had to laugh. "The schedule is like that all week." I took a deep
breath and looked longingly at my office. It's along the back wall, as is the
reception desk, but tucked behind a wall. When I was at my desk, I could
see and be seen by the staff, but not by pet parents on the other side of the
counter. On said desk there was a to-do list I'd pummeled into submission.
I rubbed my forehead and tried not to think about the amount of money
I'd spent making Lady Anthea Fitzwalter's first visit to Buckingham's a
success. Her week-long stay, topped off with the Pet Parent Appreciation
Gala, should give us financial stability, assuming any small business could
ever have that. With all the new day camp and boarding clients, not to
mention grooming appointments, my gamble was paying off.

I turned back to Dana. "We just have to keep our heads above water
this week and we'll be fine. I'll be in my office. Yell if you need me."

I made a beeline to my computer to check the status on the few
arrangements yet to be finalized. There was an email from Beach Blooms
with a photo attached. For the gala, they had initially proposed gardenia
topiaries to delineate the space on the beach and gardenia plants for
centerpieces, but gardenias were toxic to dogs. What did they have
for me this time?

How about yellow orchids and coral roses to mirror the sunset? The
photograph was of a sample on the beach at Roosevelt Inlet, at sunset.

Perfect! I wrote back.

All of the gala arrangements had fallen into place just like that. The
Event Request Form had been approved almost before the ink was dry.
The Noise Amplification Form had been signed overnight by the mayor
and city council.

I kicked my sandals off and put my feet up on my desk. I laced my
fingers behind my head and sighed. I don't know about you, but when my
nails were done and my house was clean, I felt like I could do anything.
Only one of these was the case, but that's the feeling I had. Like I could
rule the world. Of course, my house was clean. Lady Anthea had asked
if she could stay with me. My cottage-style house in a new section of
town was cozy but modest, whereas the Inn at Canal Square, in historic
downtown Lewes, was old-world elegant. It's very expensive, but each of

their seven rooms was decorated with antiques. Who wouldn't prefer that? Lady Anthea, that's who. Her own house had a name, it was Frithsden. Mine did too. It was *house*.

The walls in what we called our Sleepover Suites were decorated with photographs of the estate that she'd provided. There was one for each season. Our customer restroom had framed photos of the Frithsden gardens that looked natural and free, but at the same time planned, a feat only the English could pull off. Those images I'd lifted from the internet. Downton Abbey has nothing on Frithsden. Then there was the revelation, thanks to Wikipedia, that we had been mispronouncing the name of her estate for over a year. It wasn't Fri*th*sden, like we'd been saying, it was Friz-den. For about a month we'd all walked around repeating it, over and over, so we wouldn't slip up when we met Lady Anthea in person. Obviously, she was used to something better than my spare bedroom, but she emailed that if I had a guest room, and that if it wouldn't be too much of an imposition, that'd be A-OK with her. Actually, "brilliant" had been her word. She'd said she would enjoy getting to know me better. Truth be told, it was a lot more convenient for me. My house was in the residential area behind Buckingham's and in easy walking distance.

At five o'clock on the dot, pet parents flooded into the lobby. I could hear Dana checking out day campers. Shelby, my assistant manager, had joined her and was checking in overnight boarders.

The main phone line rang. "Buckingham Pet Palace, this is Sue Patrick."

"This is Kate Carter, Robber's mom," the voice on the other end of the line said. The eyes of her female collie mix were circled with dark brown fur, making her look like she was wearing a mask. Robber was a regular at day camp and always used our door-to-door service. Lewes was a beach town but not everyone here was on vacation. We're happy to pick a dog up from his home. For a fee, of course. I've heard of pet spas in California that use limousines. Show-offs. We're happy with a Honda van painted our signature golf-course-green with our logo. "Could you tell me what time she'll be brought home?" Kate asked.

"Henry left at the regular time. He was dropping off four dogs. Would you hold while I check to see where he is now?" I left my office and headed for the reception desk. "Shelby, have you heard from Henry?" Then I noticed she had a phone to her ear.

Shelby had been my first hire. She was forty-five, about five years older than me, and five-foot nothing. With that red hair, she may not be tall, but you wouldn't call her short. She shook her head, no, then put the phone under her chin. "It's Mr. Andrews. So-Long isn't home. He says he absolutely *must* eat at five sharp." Shelby's eyes betrayed just a hint of a roll, nothing the customers in line would notice. Then she pointed to Dana, who was on a call herself.

"Paris isn't home either," Dana stage-whispered, her shiny hair swaying. "I have Mrs. Rivard on the phone."

"I'll call Henry." I pulled my cell phone out of my pocket and speed-dialed his work cell phone. While it rang, I whispered for Dana and Shelby to tell Kate Carter, Charles Andrews, and Betsy Rivard we'd call them back. After a generous number of rings, the call went to voice mail. I knew he'd see the missed call and didn't bother to leave a message. "He's not answering. Maybe he's walking a dog in now."

The three of us took care of the remaining ten clients in line.

"Who was the fourth dog in the van?" I asked.

Shelby searched in her curly hair for her glasses, finally extricating them. "Dottie, that Dalmatian puppy, was with them. We haven't heard from Dayle Thomas. She's the pet photographer, right?" She reached over and dialed the phone.

"Yeah, I'll try Henry's cell again." No answer. Enough of hoping he'd see the missed call. "Call me, Henry!" I told his voice mail. I walked around the counter and looked out the front window. Shelby had reached Dayle Thomas, and I went back to the reception desk to get the latest update.

"Ms. Thomas says Dottie is there. She had just gotten home from her photo shoot when Henry got there."

Dana moved closer to me to whisper, "Where is she?" She motioned to the large photograph of Lady Anthea Fitzwalter seated on what looked like an antique bench, ankles crossed, and flanked by two of her corgis. She was the centerpiece of the painting, but the bottom half of an ornately framed portrait of one of her ancestors could be seen over her shoulders.

"She's at my house." I dialed my van driver again. Nothing. "She's freshening up." Why did I just say that? I hate it. It implies you were something else before. All I know is, it's a phrase you don't want to overthink.

The bay window of our gift shop gave a better view of the side parking lot, empty except for my Jeep and Shelby's Prius.

Shelby raised an eyebrow. "She's probably running up your phone bill, making international phone calls to her idiot brother, the duke." There was a lull with no clients, so Shelby could speak loud enough for me to hear from the store where I was straightening a row of tiara chew toys. We *may* have Googled Lady Anthea's brother. We may have done it a lot.

Dana giggled. "That's harsh."

"Can either of you explain to me how he can make the same speech at every charity event and museum opening he goes to, and still not speak in complete sentences?" Shelby taught high school English until she had quit in a blaze of glory. She and her husband, who had been an analyst on Wall Street, visited our ocean one Christmas break and they never went back. She took a job walking dogs and realized she liked their personalities better than those of the children she'd been teaching.

"When Lady Anthea gets here, remember that we know nothing about her brother."

The phone rang and I was back in reception in a flash. Shelby covered the receiver with her palm. "It's chief somebody. He needs to talk to you."

"Huh?" I cocked my head from one side to the other, the way Abby does when she hears something she wants to understand but can't quite make out.

Shelby shrugged her shoulders. She didn't know who it was either.

"Is it something you can handle?"

She looked around to be sure there were no pet parents in the lobby and answered. Then she put the call on speaker. "This is Shelby Ryan. Can I…."

There was a roar over the line. "I AM CHIEF JOHN TURNER OF THE LEWES POLICE DEPARTMENT!" The man took a breath and I could hear dogs barking in the background. I had a visceral reaction to the distress I heard. "Your van was found abandoned in a line of cars leading to the Cape May-Lewes Ferry terminal parking lot. I am two seconds away from having the door forcibly removed."

"No!"

"No!"

"No!"

"No!"

Math's never been my strong suit, but there were three of us and four no's. I glanced up at Dana and Shelby. Their mouths were in O's and they were fixated on something over my right shoulder. Slowly I turned.

"Lady Anthea?" I reached my hand out to shake hers.

This was our first in-person meeting. I knew from her bio that she was about my age. And, like the picture in my head, she wore a knee-length skirt with a blazer. These were blue, accessorized by the Hermès scarf tied around her neck along with sensible pumps. Her eyes swept over the three of us dressed in khaki Bermuda shorts and green tops with Buckingham's logo. We were wearing our polo shirts, our summer uniform. In the fall we'd switch to button-down oxford shirts. I wasn't prepared for the raised eyebrow, nor the mouth in a hard, straight line.

Whatever. I ran to my office for my handbag—which is really a beach bag—and grabbed the keys on the plastic peg shaped like a dog's tail. I yelled at the phone, "I'm on my way. I'll be there in five." It would take me ten minutes. I motioned for Shelby to disconnect the call. "Shelby, call the DRBA police desk in the ferry terminal. Ask for Wayne. Tell him I'll buy him a drink if he stops this. Dana, keep trying Henry's cell."

As I ran by Anthea, it occurred to me that she might be able to help. What's the use of having a local celebrity if they can't get you and your dogs out of a jam? Without slowing down, I grabbed her arm. "Come with me."

Chapter 2

I pulled out of the Villages of Five Points community and, in one of those little gifts from the universe, caught a green light to make the left onto Savannah Road. My passenger was silent. Our two-year-old partnership was the result of a project by Global She, an international organization of female small business owners, to encourage collaboration among women from different cultures. I'm not sure we're what they had in mind, but it's worked.

I was born and raised in Lewes but hadn't lived here since I went away to college in Georgia. After graduation I worked as a dog walker, sitter, and trainer in one East Coast beach town after another. I had never stayed more than a couple of years in any of them. When I was thirty-six, I came home to Lewes. I was ready for the next phase of my life to begin. I wanted to open a pet daycare and boarding facility, with lots of frills. But mostly, I wanted to stay.

I knew a lot about caring for dogs, but I needed something to make my business stand out. I needed help with branding. Lady Anthea Fitzwalter was offering her consulting services. I sent her an email with my proposal and offered a percentage of the profits. For years, I'd read about this or that royal being a charity's patron, and that was what I had in mind. She wrote back right away with her approval and the "pet-ronage" began.

To make conversation, I pointed to the local veterinary clinic, Lewes 24-Hour Pet Care.

"That's nice to have a surgery so close by. Does the veterinarian make house calls?"

"Thankfully we've never needed him to. Our staff and his get along great."

"But you and he don't?"

Time for honesty. "Dr. Walton hates me. And our pet resort. A few months ago he stopped offering boarding and day care because we've taken 90 percent of his business."

I glanced over to read her reaction. She was smiling. "Why only 90 percent?"

We both laughed. Then she said, "I appreciate your emails apprising me of all aspects of the enterprise. Why do you think it's been such a success?"

"We have something special. That's you. And I try to provide extras the pet parents want. For instance, Lewes has its share of retirees, and when we bought the van, the non-drivers became a source of new business, both for camp and grooming. We charge for pickup and drop-off for day camp, but not for bringing the dogs in for boarding or grooming."

She nodded and then leaned back and seemed to enjoy the sights. We passed shops and restaurants as we drove through the first town in the first state. "Delaware was the first state to ratify the Constitution, and Lewes was the first settlement in Delaware," I explained. I told her city was founded in 1631, and other historical particulars.

"Lewes is in Sussex County, just like Lewes, England," she said.

"Someone's done her homework," I said.

She didn't respond, and we drove in an uncomfortable silence for a bit. Was even that gentle bid of teasing too familiar?

We crossed the canal bridge and just before the Lewes beach, I turned right onto Cape Henlopen Drive. This street ends at one of the country's first open spaces, the five-thousand-acre Cape Henlopen State Park. But we weren't going that far.

"You'll give your driver a talking to when we get there?" she asked finally.

"If he's there. They found the van, not Henry."

She must have realized then that we wouldn't need to unlock the vehicle if Henry was around because she murmured an apology. We were going to get the dogs out and back to their homes. We still had to locate Henry.

In a few minutes, she spoke again. "Do you think he may have, to quote some of the young people we've employed at home, done a runner?"

I shrugged. Truth was, because it was Henry we were talking about, I had no idea.

Sure enough, the Buckingham van was on the street, in line to turn into the parking lot and go through a ticket stall. Just waiting there surrounded by the white Lewes police cars, parked at a respectful distance, like suitors and a debutante. A Lewes police officer directed traffic headed farther down Cape Henlopen Drive to the far-right lane. Wayne waved me around to enter the ferry parking lot through a closed ticket booth, and motioned for me to park at the curb. As I passed, he gave a lazy salute, then mouthed Gilligan's. I wondered why he had chosen that restaurant for me to pay up at, instead of On The Rocks, the outdoor bar at the ferry terminal he usually preferred. It was all good. Lady Anthea and I could have dinner at Gilligan's after I'd settled my debt to buy him a drink.

One of the ferries had docked and cars waited to drive onto the ramp. Their passengers gawked at the hive of police activity back on the street, but the drivers had to pay attention. There was another delay before the cars could drive onto the ferry for the seventeen-mile, eighty-five-minute crossing. The cars were stopped at a spot farther along the route to the waiting ferry, where a bomb-sniffing dog, a powerful and attentive German Shepherd, walked up and down the line, and an officer with a mirror checked undercarriages. Almost everything had changed at the fifty-year-old ferry after 9/11. The Delaware River and Bay Authority operates the Cape May-Lewes Ferry, among other transportation links between Delaware and New Jersey. Both the DRBA Police Department, made up of officers like Wayne, and the City of Lewes Police, would want to know why a van had been abandoned just outside a parking lot full of a few hundred people.

I parked and took a couple of steps toward the action before I realized Lady Anthea hadn't moved. "If you'd rather wait in the car..." I held out my hand with the car keys. She could listen to either the Elvis or the Jimmy Buffett satellite radio station.

"I should go with you." She took a deep breath and got out of the car.

We backtracked to the street and looked around at all the purposeful chaos. It wasn't hard to tell who was in charge. Chief John Turner was tall, maybe as tall as Dana, but then she's a model. He was new, so I had never met him, but I certainly liked him better when he wasn't yelling. The whimsically painted mini-van was in sharp contrast to his severe demeanor and uniform. Said uniform wasn't particularly stern, being a light blue, short-sleeve shirt and navy pants. It was somewhere between late afternoon and early evening, which placed the sun behind him, outlining his broad build. I guess the way we'd been let through told him who we were because he left the group of uniformed officers he'd been talking to. We watched each other through matching Ray-Bans and met up at the back of the Honda.

He gave me his name then reached out and we shook hands.

"I'm Sue Patrick and this is Lady Anthea Fitzwalter."

She stared at his outstretched hand for a beat. It seemed an eternity—like what her formality was going to make this week feel like—before she relaxed and shook his hand.

"Nice to meet you," he said. I'd place his age in the mid-forties. He looked like he'd spent a lot of time outdoors. "You're from the dog place?" He had to speak loud enough to be heard over the barking coming from inside the van.

"The Pet Palace," I corrected him.

Suddenly, the barking stopped.

"The what?" Turner said with a raised eyebrow and a curled lip. He glanced back at the now quiet van.

Lady Anthea cleared her throat to regain his attention and pointed to the burgundy lettering on the van. "We're the owners of the Buckingham Pet Palace."

Turner turned back to us. Derision oozed out of the police chief's pores, making me feel like the 1950s Elvis surrounded by a congregation of Southern Baptists. He opened his mouth to say something, and the barking started again. A small dog first, a larger dog joining in. And the third rounding out the harmony.

"Uh, I have the key," I said. The van went silent again. "Can I open the door now?"

He held up a stop-sign hand. "Juuuust a second." His voice was deep, almost a growl. He scanned the parking lot, stopping when he saw the handler of the German Shepherd. Then he spoke into the radio on his shoulder. "Chuck?" The handler looked our way and the dog lowered to a ready sit. From this position, he could jump up in less than a second. Chief Turner motioned for him, actually them, to join us and spoke into his radio again. "Can you give this another check?"

We watched and waited as the dog handler and the German Shepherd wove through the cars to get to us.

The pleasantries were out of the way, and we were about to see how long he would think it was nice to meet me. "There are three dogs in that vehicle and it's August. I'm responsible for them and I need to open that door right away." Water bowls were attached to the rungs on the sides of the crates and the dogs sounded okay, but since mentioning either fact would hurt my case, I didn't.

"Animals in a closed-up car is something we take very seriously," Lady Anthea said. She was standing beside me, and it felt good to have her support.

The police chief took in my face and then hers. "I need just another minute."

Another minute? No. I pointed the key fob at the van.

"Please." Turner's voice was unexpectedly gentle. I lowered my arm and took a deep breath.

I turned to Lady Anthea. "I know the dog handler, Chuck. There used to be a children's daycare center in the Villages of Five Points. He and I gave a talk to the kids there and they met one of his dogs. They're all cross-trained in bomb sniffing and attack. The dogs, that is. Not the kids. But maybe they are too, I wouldn't know." Before he could stop himself, Chief Turner laughed. I went on. "We didn't mention the attack part to them." I got a kick out of seeing him loosen up, but I was also rambling to hide my rising anxiety about the dogs.

When Chuck got closer, his dog turned in a circle either from excitement or confusion. The Shepherd walked around the back of the van and halfway up the length of the vehicle, then reversed and walked back to the middle of the van on the other side. When they passed our little group, the handler said, "Hi, Sue." Then he turned to Chief Turner. "There's an unfamiliar scent coming from the back of the van."

"He's not just reacting to the dogs in there?" I asked.

Chuck shrugged his shoulders. "Could be, but I don't think so."

"So are we cleared to open the vehicle?" Chief Turner asked.

"Go ahead." The two men said goodbye via that reverse-nod motion their gender uses. Chuck and his dog went back to inspecting cars lined up to drive onto the ferry.

I went around to the side of the van and Lady Anthea followed.

"Those dogs gonna leap out?" Chief Turner leaned over me as I clicked the key fob, and the side door rolled back.

"No, they're in crates." I had my foot on the running board about to step in. The dogs went silent and stiffened as the door opened. All three—the dachshund, the collie mix, and the poodle—were on high alert, getting information from wherever they could. Seeing, smelling, or hearing. "It's okay, fellas." Their backs and tails relaxed. Robber's front legs bent a little. The crates squeaked as they shifted their weight, moving their paws up and down as they calmed. Paris sighed and gave a little "mmm" whimper.

"Everything's fine."

Only it wasn't. There was something on the floor, between the two rows of crates. My employee, Henry. The front of his white undershirt was covered in black blood. His eyes were open and his chin was raised. He seemed to be looking to his side, or over his shoulder. His right arm was bent at the elbow, with his lower arm either protecting his throat, or the lower part of his face. I backed out of the van, thinking my shoe would never reach the asphalt. "Chief?"

I'm five-foot-seven, but he bent forward to hear me. I tilted my head to the van's interior. The dogs, all three, were still watching me. Waiting for me. As I was processing what I'd seen, I was raising a wall so this couldn't hurt me.

Turner leaned in and saw what I had seen. He radioed for another officer to join him, then he took off his sunglasses and looked at me. "I'm sorry. That explains Chuck's dog's confusion. He's not trained to detect a cadaver." Then he turned to the uniformed woman. "Get a crime scene team out here."

A corpse, outside of a funeral, should have scared me. Instead, I was enormously sad. Henry was my latest hire. He had worked at Buckingham's for three months but was still outside the team we had become. The confident, dynamic man I interviewed turned out to be arrogant and cagey. I was planning to fire him, but that didn't change the fact that I hadn't been there to take care of my employee. I found myself mentally promising him that we'd find out who did this. We?

I looked over at Lady Anthea standing ramrod stiff. "Henry? Is he...?" she asked.

I nodded, looking down at my feet.

She cleared her throat. If anything, she pulled herself up even taller, straighter, and more in control. Then she asked me, "Can we get the dogs out? We need to take them to their respective homes."

Chief Turner's eyes darted to the van, but he didn't answer.

I turned to him. "With some help, we can take the crates out the back of the van, and not disturb anything."

Finally, he said, "All right, but can you take the animals and leave the crates? I'm concerned there might be blood spatter on them."

"Sure." I had read enough murder mysteries to know what blood spatter was. Just last night I had finished *Murder, My Dear* and planned to begin drawing the secrets out of *Assassins Aren't Angels*—or maybe the title was *Angels Aren't Assassins*—later that evening.

"Would you pull the Jeep over here?" I asked Lady Anthea.

"Certainly."

I handed her the keys, and she turned and marched back to my car.

She went first to the passenger side, then corrected. I hoped Chief Turner hadn't noticed. No such luck.

Turner touched my elbow. "Was that a good idea?"

"She'll be fine. She's in a parking lot, so she doesn't have to worry about which lane to use."

We walked to the rear of the van, and I raised the door. Anthea drove back to the street without incident. Then she backed the Jeep up to us until I called out, "Okay, that's close enough."

Chief Turner pulled me away from the van, and I instinctively yanked my arm back.

"Brake! Brake!" I yelled.

Every cloud has a silver lining. She wasn't accelerating when she collided with the van, so she rolled into it. "Considering she's probably never driven an automatic transmission car in her life, not bad," I said to Chief Turner as I waited for Anthea to climb out of the Jeep. I took her place and pulled my vehicle forward a few feet and got out.

I turned to Anthea. "I'm not wild about driving with dogs loose in the car, but I don't think we have a choice. I have a harness we can use for Robber."

"I can sit with the dachshund and the miniature poodle in my lap," she offered. "Are their leads in the van? I'm sure they'll need walks." I didn't know if Chief Turner understood that *walk* was a euphemism for going to the bathroom, but I knew that's what she meant. She seemed happy to be of service that didn't involve driving in the States, in what to her was the wrong side of the car.

Chief Turner was shaking his head. "Sorry, that van is a crime scene now. Anything in there, other than those dogs, has to stay."

"The only leash I have in the Jeep is Abby's," I said.

"That's fine. If we can't get the leads from the van, I'll just take them one at a time."

I took a deep breath. I'd have to get the dogs to her before she could start taking them to relieve themselves. After steeling myself, I climbed into the van. At least two of the dogs could be handed out the rear door. The dachshund would come out first. I awkwardly straddled Henry's legs, careful not to touch his pristine deck shoes or his blue jeans. I leaned over and opened the door to So-Long's crate, careful to keep the wire door from touching the body. Once I had him out, I held him close and backed up. I kissed the top of his head before twisting around and positioning myself to lower him down to Lady Anthea's waiting arms. Suddenly all four of his feet were scrambling in an attempt to stay attached to me. "It's okay," I whispered.

Lady Anthea snapped her fingers at him. "We'll have none of that, young man!" I handed the dog down, and she walked over and deposited him into the back seat of the Jeep. We repeated the maneuver—no finger snapping needed this time—for Paris, the miniature French poodle. Robber's crate was behind the driver's seat. The doors to the crates faced the van's center aisle, and I inched forward then stepped over Henry's shoulders. I stood straddling Henry's head and neck, wondering how the hell I was going to get a seventy-five-pound dog out of there, without any of his four feet touching the floor. I looked at Robber for—oh I don't know, maybe some guidance or a little I-know-you-can-do-it energy. The collie stopped pacing long enough to give me a blank stare. She seemed mildly curious to see what I would come up with. The longer I stalled, the more fidgety she grew.

"Sue," Lady Anthea called, "the bitch needs to know you're in charge."

I leaned closer to Robber. "You know she was referring to your gender, right?" The dog was so anxious to get out that I was sure she'd lunge for freedom as soon as the crate door opened. Chief Turner was watching me from the still open side door. The side door! That's how I would get her out. I carefully rotated myself, reversing so I was facing the back of the van. I took a deep breath and opened the crate door. "Go!"

Robber jumped out and I caught her mid-air, with both of my arms under her ribcage. If I lived to be a hundred years old, I would never forget the look on Chief Turner's face when he saw the airborne dog flying his way. Then his expression when he realized I had caught the animal and that he wasn't going to die. I moved my right leg over Henry's body and sidestepped to the door. Lady Anthea met us there. She gently pulled Chief Turner, who was imitating a statue, out of the way. I let Robber jump down from the van. Lady Anthea grabbed her collar and held on. Abby's leash was hanging from her shoulder and with her free hand she hooked it to the dog. We allowed ourselves a quick smile for our victory. She led Robber to a nearby grassy island, where she promptly relieved herself.

When Chief Turner was able to speak again, he said, "I need the name and phone number of the victim's next of kin."

"Looks like what you need is a drink," I said. I pulled my cell phone out of my pants pocket and hit speed dial for Buckingham's. Shelby answered and I told her about Henry. Ignoring Turner's scowl, I gave her a minute to digest the bad news before I asked her to look in Henry's personnel folder.

She told Dana that she had to go to my office, then said to me, "Be right back."

Being put on hold gave me a chance to think about what had happened. Every muscle in my body was clenched, and my heart was still racing. I don't know one piece of classical music from another, and I was praying what I was listening to wasn't the one where they fire a canon at the end. If it was, I would probably drop dead on the spot.

"You're on hold?" Turner asked.

"No," I lied. Then I made un-huh noises into the phone. Thanks to my recent close reading of *The Killer Wore a Kilt*, I knew the police liked to control the release of information on a case. He was going to give me a hard time for telling Shelby about Henry's death, and if I pretended like I was still talking, I could put it off. Maybe he'd forget.

"You know I can hear the hold music, right?"

Giving up my pretend exchange, I said, "I trust Shelby. And I didn't want to have to lie to her about why I needed the phone number."

"Tell her not to tell anyone."

While I waited for the information, I watched Lady Anthea walk Robber to the Jeep. She commanded the dog to jump into the rear of the car and she did, no questions asked. Then she leashed So-Long and took him over to the spot Robber had christened. By then I was ready to dictate the number, which the chief noted on his tablet. "He gave his sister as his closest relative. Her name is Ashley Trent and she lives in Albany, New York." I asked Shelby to text me the addresses for our three passengers, and to tell the pet parents we were on our way.

"How does this work?" he asked, still typing.

I looked at him, wondering what kind of idiot the city had hired. "Well, somebody killed somebody and now you figure out who did it. Does that sound about right?"

His head jerked up. "That's hardly what I was asking. Do your customers pay for these rides?" He motioned to the van.

"Sure."

"Would your driver have been carrying money?"

"No." I shook my head. "We have credit card numbers on file. All of the door-to-door services are paid that way. There are very few cash transactions for anything."

"Did your employee wear anything someone might want to steal, like an expensive watch or jewelry?"

"No," I answered.

"Do you know if he carried large amounts of cash in his wallet?"

"I wouldn't know," I said. "I never saw him flashing any...." I let the sentence drift, and I turned to look over the top of the ferry building to the ocean. It was obvious the line of questioning was about a possible motive for Henry's murder.

"Or drugs?"

I tilted my head back to Chief Turner. "Not that I ever saw or even suspected. I have no idea why anyone would do this."

The chief nodded and went back to doing whatever police chiefs do when someone's been murdered. His questions had made me uneasy about what the days ahead would bring, what we would learn about Henry and about our world.

Already the Buckingham van was surrounded by orange cones and four or five law enforcement officers. Two Lewes police cars, which for all I knew could be the totality of the force's fleet, had been moved closer. The cheerful yellow swirls painted on their car doors now seemed unbefitting to me, and I turned my head.

Next, Paris had her turn for doing her business and she performed admirably. Lady Anthea got in the passenger seat and I placed both the smaller dogs on her lap. As I closed the door, I looked back to see the woman police officer picking sand and gravel out of the Buckingham van's tire treads and bagging it. I pulled my eyes away.

"Our first stop will be to drop off the dachshund. Charles Andrews swears the dog has low blood sugar."

"Does he?" Anthea looked the dog in the eye; it seemed she dared him to tell a fib. He pulled back. "I've never heard of such a thing."

"We checked with his vet to confirm that he doesn't have diabetes. He doesn't."

I took back roads to Route 1 and we headed south toward Rehoboth Beach. In a few miles we turned left, back toward the water. We hadn't been talking. Again, Lady Anthea seemed to be taking in as much of the scenery as she could.

"Here's Charles's street. I hope you haven't been too uncomfortable holding both dogs."

"Not at all. Do you think anyone will complain about the dogs riding in the front seat unsecured?"

"Once they know they're in your lap, it'll be fine," I assured her.

Charles Andrews came out of his house before we had come to a complete stop. How was I going to explain where So-Long's leash was? Turns out I didn't have to. Anthea opened the car door and the eighty-year-old widower reached for his dog, easily taking him into his arms. "Are you okay?"

"Oh, maybe a touch of jet lag," Lady Anthea said.

"I'm fine just a little sho....," I said. Mr. Andrews was holding the dachshund close and looking into his eyes. It was obvious he hadn't been asking about either of us. "Oh, you were talking to So-Long."

"Yes, I was. I heard what happened. Or almost happened."

"Almost?" My intention was to say as little as possible, but Henry wasn't almost dead.

"Sue, I trusted you. And now I hear your employee was killed trying to steal our dogs."

"Where did you hear that?" I asked, trying not to get annoyed.

"From an extremely reliable source." You can't throw a stick in a small town like Lewes without hitting a so-called reliable source.

As much as I wanted to know who had made such an outlandish suggestion about my employee, I didn't have time to cajole it out of Charles Andrews. We had two more dogs to deliver. "Let's wait until all the facts come out."

He continued to examine his dog for ill effects. So-Long's expression hadn't changed. "May I introduce you to Lady Anthea Fitzwalter?"

That drew his attention from the dog, but not for long. "Pleasure to meet you." Then he went back to scrutinizing his dog.

She smiled. "The pleasure is all mine."

"See you Friday night," I called on my way back to the Jeep.

"I don't..." The rest of what Charles had to say was lost in a mumble.

"I do hope so, Mr. Andrews," Lady Anthea said. "I always say it's not summer without an annual fête." Was it possible she had just sounded more British?

"Well, I guess I'll be there." Allowing himself to be charmed into relenting, but only to a maybe.

I said good night and we headed out for our next drop off. "He seemed to be having second thoughts about coming to the gala. And I know he had really been looking forward to it."

"I'm sure everything will be fine by Friday. This is only Monday."

***

"My poor baby! Almost a Canadian!" Kate Carter leaned into the back seat of the Jeep and hugged Robber.

Huh?

"Sue, I heard all about it. You must be so relieved he didn't get away with it."

For the time being, Henry's killer *had* gotten away with it. I had known Kate, fifty-something, blond, tall, but she always wore heels, throwing safety to the wind for years. She read the confusion on my face. "You don't know?"

I opened the rear passenger side door and a worn-out Robber lumbered down. "Know what?" Oh, I knew plenty.

Kate ran her hand down the back of her sleepy dog's neck. "Your employee was on his way to Canada to sell our dogs. Somebody, must have been a dog person, committed murder to stop him. I hope you don't have any other rogue employees like that. I've never heard anything like it."

"Neither have I," the British voice in the front seat said.

Lady Anthea got out and patted the startled dog owner's arm. "Certainly, we can't be too careful with our dogs."

Kate was about to say something but Lady Anthea rolled on.

"The queen's favorite corgi breeder is also my breeder." Let's just say, she didn't have to worry about Kate interrupting again. That line was a showstopper. "Our corgis are from the same line. My two are being boarded at her farm while I'm here in the..." She hesitated. This was going to be good. Oh, no. What if she pulled out one of her obscure cultural references? "...The *colonies*." She bestowed a smile, and Kate looked like she wished she had a notepad on her. "Buckingham Pet Palace is as safe as a dog can be. You have my word."

"Thank yooooou," Kate reverently whispered.

I couldn't move. I had never seen anything like that performance. I was grateful. I'm not sure what the political parties are in England, but at that moment I would have voted for anyone my business partner wanted me to. Tories? Do they still have Tories?

I moved Paris from the driver's seat, where Anthea had deposited her, and started the Jeep. I had to get Lady Anthea away from there before Kate started curtsying. We had one more stop before we could return to Lewes.

* * * *

I accelerated onto Route 1. We were both happy to have all three dogs safely in their own homes and to be heading back to Lewes for dinner. Betsy Rivard had the same crazy story about Henry intending to sell the dogs, and Anthea had charmed her the same way as the others. Of course, she felt her poodle, Paris, was the real target of the scheme.

"Is the weather always this pleasant?" she asked.

"The weather in Delaware is pretty mild. And this summer has been especially nice. We have the occasional tropical storm and nor'easter, but none are predicted this month. The weather should be perfect for Friday's gala. Want to stop by the Lewes beach to watch the sunset before going to Gilligan's?"

"Oh, yes! That would be lovely."

I looked at the clock on the dash. "I just need to call Buckingham's to check on everyone." She cringed and I realized I had said Buckingham's. That's what all our pet parents call it, but Anthea hates it. Was she afraid someone would confuse the palace in London with a pet resort in Lewes, Delaware?

After a quick chat with Shelby, I had been assured the two overnight employees had fed all the boarders and most of the dogs were ready for bed. Dana had fed Abby and walked her to my house, before going home for the night. I told her about the crazy rumor that had spread so quickly. "Who could have started it?" Shelby asked. "Only the police, Lady Anthea, and you know about Henry's murder, right? I told our people what I knew, but I don't think any of them would embellish it."

Neither of us spoke. We didn't need to. The only Buckingham staffer that would play fast and loose with the truth like that was Henry.

Anthea and I headed down Savannah Road to Lewes Beach at its end. A handful of cars were lined up facing the ocean. "About half of these people are vacationers. After Labor Day, only locals will come here."

"When is that?"

"It's the first weekend of September." I parked but didn't budge. It felt good to be still. "Most of the regulars who come here at this time of day are retirees and a lot of them are our clients."

"I think it's a good idea for the people here in the car park to see you and, if necessary, hear you refute that nonsense about their dogs being abducted."

"After the day we've had, I'd rather have an early night."

"It'll help restore confidence. Uneasy lies the head that wears a crown."

I looked over at her.

"Shakespeare," she said.

"Thank you."

"*Henry IV*, specifically."

"I meant, thank you for stepping up when we dropped off the dogs," I said. "You charmed their socks off."

"I was laying it on a little thick, don't you think?" She laughed at herself, but I had heard pride in a job well done in her voice.

"I wonder how many people will decide they have other plans for Friday night?" I looked through the windshield at the ocean, like it could tell me the future.

"What about *after* Friday night?" Lady Anthea's question brought me out of my daze. "Could Henry's murder irreparably damage the confidence the town has in the business?"

"Not if I can help it." I opened the car door. "'Courage is being scared to death and saddling up anyway.' That was John Wayne."

She got out and followed me to the white, sandy beach. Some of the sunset watchers were enjoying ice cream cones from the Dairy Queen across the street. Hopkins Farm ice cream is from a dairy farm on Route 9 and was also an excellent choice, but for convenience you couldn't beat DQ. This gentle ritual of our small beach town was certainly more to my taste than the rumor mill that had our clients' dogs emigrating to Canada. A light wind swirled the sugary sand around the asphalt, making and unmaking one design after another. If I caught the eye of anyone in a car, I waved. I introduced Anthea to three couples sitting on the white, wooden benches where the parking lot met the beach.

"Want to walk a little?" I asked.

"Brilliant!" she said.

I pulled off my sandals. "Uh-oh." I had forgotten that she was wearing pantyhose and heels. I pointed to the Beach Patrol office. "There's a restroom in there if you want to change."

"No worries." It was obvious she had no intention of removing her shoes. She began walking and I scrambled to catch up.

"Where are the waves I've heard so much about?" she asked.

"Lewes Beach is on the bay. Our town is at the mouth of the Delaware Bay." Then I pointed east to the series of low, rock walls extending out from the shore and the two lighthouses. "That's our breakwater. On the other side is the Atlantic Ocean where the waves are. The breakwaters reduce the intensity of the waves and provide safe harbor."

"Safe harbor," she repeated. I wondered if they used a different term in England.

We walked down the shoreline, and I introduced her to other beach walkers. She made conversation comparing US beaches to those in England. Suddenly she gasped. "Look!" she yelled and pointed to the western sky. "We almost missed the sunset."

Chapter 3

Gilligan's Waterfront Restaurant overlooked the Lewes-Rehoboth Canal that cut through downtown Lewes. Before its major renovation it looked like a boat used as a bar, with a restaurant that had seemingly sprouted from it. Wayne was at the bar when we walked in, wearing jeans and a mostly yellow Hawaiian shirt. He smiled and held up a beer mug. I was hoping I hadn't started anything I had no interest in pursuing. Surely, he knew if I wanted to date him, I would have by now. He was surrounded by a couple I knew from the Lighthouse Foundation Board and a couple I knew from surfing. If you can call what we do at Cape Henlopen surfing. Mostly we sit on our boards, joking around and talking about nothing. This was the town that had welcomed me back after my years of roaming.

"You're about as far out of uniform as you can get." I pointed at Wayne's flip-flops and laughed. He laughed back. "I thought you'd be working overtime."

He shrugged his broad shoulders. "For now, the case is being handled by the city police. Lucky for us, it happened on the street instead of at the ferry terminal." That unapologetic lack of ambition was part of his charm.

"Let me introduce Lady Anthea Fitzwalter."

Wayne transferred his beer to his left hand, dried his right on his jeans, and then held it out to her. She smiled and then pumped it up and down with such vigor that his beer sloshed. Obviously this was all unfamiliar to her, but she was making a when-in-Rome effort. Considering she was only here for a week, then she'd be gone, I appreciated it. Next I introduced Barb and Red Moulinier from the Lighthouse Foundation, and the surfers, Jerry and his wife, Charlie. All four put their drinks on the bar before submitting to Anthea's athletic grip.

Wayne turned to talk to Jerry and Charlie about the repair work being done on the Harbor of Refuge Lighthouse, and Barb and Red moved closer to me and Lady Anthea. Red tilted his head toward Wayne. "Why won't you go out with him?"

"Yeah, what could possibly be wrong with *him*?" Barb ran her eyes up and down Wayne's pretty darn close to perfect body and giggled.

"Easy, now," her husband of forty years said.

"I know him too well," I said.

Barb looked at Lady Anthea. "That's a new one. There was the guy whose hands were too small. The guy that mispronounced potpourri. The guy who used air quotes."

Red picked up the list of the reasons I had ended, or never begun, relationships. "The guy with teeth that were too white."

"Time to change the subject," I said. I turned to Lady Anthea. "Red and Barb are finding musicians for the gala."

Red pulled a business card out of his shirt pocket and presented it to Lady Anthea. "It's just something we started after we retired."

"He's being modest. They run the best booking agency in southern Delaware. Every other event in Lewes uses them."

"We aim to please," Red said in an aw-shucks way. "We found your classical guitarist. Can we talk about that other matter?"

"An Elvis impersonator? Still, no."

Barb reached out a hand to me. "Sue, we were just thinking you could sing a duet with someone."

"You sing?" Lady Anthea sounded surprised.

"Maybe. A little," I said. "But not with Elvis impersonators." Just to be clear.

Red looked at Barb. "You can't say we didn't try." He turned to me. "The guitarist will play while the guests eat, then you'll sing, if we can find someone who is not an Elvis impersonator to sing with you, and then the disc jockey will play Elvis music for everyone to dance to on the beach."

"Perfect!" I said.

Lady Anthea began laughing and took a step back, bumping someone. "Oh, pardon me."

A slight, older man with thinning hair and a gentle smile had joined the crowd at the bar. I'd seen him around town but never met him. "It was my fault entirely," he said.

Actually, it was. I wouldn't have said so for the world, but he had moved in right behind her.

He held out his hand to shake hers, and my eyes automatically went to his drink. It was in a safe zone. "Peter Collins." Brown eyes twinkled behind his round eyeglasses.

"Anthea Fitzwalter."

"Is that a British accent I hear?"

"Yes." To allay the fears of the pet parents she'd played super-duper British all night. Now her one-word answer made me think she was tired of it. "Do you live in Lewes?" she asked him to shift the conversation.

He took a sip of his cocktail. "I recently retired here from the cellular phone industry." Then he turned to me. "You're Sue Patrick, right? And you own Buckingham Pet Palace if I'm not mistaken."

I smiled then pointed at Lady Anthea. "We're co-owners. And you own the new antiques store on Second Avenue?"

"Guilty as charged," he said with a chuckle. "I was on a buying trip to Manhattan just today." He turned his attention back to Lady Anthea. "The Best of the Past is the name of my little shop. It's an antiques store and art gallery combined."

"Do you specialize in a particular period?" Lady Anthea asked.

When Collins hesitated in answering, I said, "I'll go put our name in for a table." I turned a little too quick and ran into a wall. With arms. Which reached out to steady me. "Chief Turner, how tall are you?" I asked. I had almost called him Chief Tall Drink.

"Tall enough."

"Sorry, I meant to say how *are* you." I really had misspoken. The serious buzzkill look on his face took away any fleeting inclination I may have had to tease him. He was in uniform—he seemed like the kind of guy who was always in uniform. His thick black hair had a little gray at the temples. He'd pocketed his Ray-Bans, and I saw that his eyes were blue. His tanned face was lined more by the sun than a lot of years. My forty-something estimate for his age stood.

"I saw your Jeep parked out front." Something in his tone sounded like an apology, so I assumed I was about to get a ticket. Lord knows it wouldn't be my first. "Can we talk?"

He walked away without waiting for an answer.

"Good to see you, Mr. Collins," I said. The chief could wait.

Lady Anthea smiled at the antiques store owner, seconding my motion. "Any menu recommendations?" she asked him.

He gave the room a supercilious once-over, as if he smelled something bad. "I consider myself somewhat of a gourmet, so I'm not the best person to ask."

Chief Turner was standing at the open door leading out to the deck. I'd made him wait long enough. "Would you excuse us, Mr. Collins?" I pulled her arm, and when we were out of earshot, I whispered, "He's not with the health department, so I don't care what he thinks. Everything on the menu is good."

She nodded that she'd heard me. I thought Chief Turner was going to lead me outside for our confab, but we stayed there blocking the doorway. He scanned the room before he spoke. "We reached Ms. Trent." The way he said the name should have alerted me that there was more to the story, and it would have if I hadn't been getting tired. "She's not Henry's sister. She's his fiancée, and for some reason she was very annoyed with us for getting that wrong."

"As in engaged to be married? I mean, he planned to go back to Albany? Upstate New York is so far away."

"Yes, she says he came here to take a job with you." I probably imagined the emphasis on the last two words. "Says he works such long hours they haven't seen very much of each other since he took the job. And not at all in the last month."

"Long hours?" Before I knew it, I was speaking ill of the dead. "We're talking about Henry Cannon, right?" Turner didn't answer; I hadn't expected him to. "I wonder why he never mentioned her?" I looked out into the night, like there might just be an answer out there. Or not.

"You can ask her tomorrow, when she comes to identify the body." That brought me back. "I can?"

"No, I didn't mean that literally. Also, the number he gave you wasn't a working number."

I shrugged. "Wait, maybe it was when he filled out the employment application three months ago. Have you thought about that?"

"The area code was wrong for Albany, New York. I had my administrative assistant find Ashley Trent."

"You're implying he intentionally gave a bogus emergency contact? Why would he, or anyone else, do that?" I felt like he was blaming the victim, and doing it awfully early. "I have something to ask you. A rumor started almost immediately that Henry had stolen the dogs. One pet parent even said he was taking them to Canada to sell them! How did word get out about the murder *within the hour*, and how did that crazy rumor get started?"

"Not from my office, if that's what *you're* implying. And what makes you so sure he wasn't about to drive that van onto the ferry?"

"Well, for one thing, he wasn't in the driver's seat."

"He could have been when he drove up." Both of the chief's hands were in his pockets, and he was doing that leaning over me thing.

I gave him what I hoped came across as a sarcastic smile and raised the collar of my Buckingham Pet Palace polo shirt. "Where is his shirt? He was wearing it when he left Buckingham's."

I shook my head because I wasn't ready for the image my mind had started playing and replaying of Henry leaving with the last of the four dogs. Shelby, who had helped him load the van, said something to him and he'd snarled, "Later," without looking back.

I realized I had closed my eyes and snapped back to the here and now. Turner was really invading my space. "You're in luck."

He straightened and ran a hand over his hair. "How do you figure that?"

"The ticket stalls have security cameras," I said.

"The van didn't enter the parking lot," Chief Turner said, "but, who knows, maybe the range of the closest one will include at least some of the street outside."

"There's an outside camera at the far end of the stalls. It would provide coverage of Cape Henlopen Drive, wouldn't it?" I looked back at Wayne. No one from DRBA had told the new guy in town, Chief Turner, about that last camera.

"Sue, are you saying a CCTV camera could show someone wearing his uniform shirt to the ferry?" Lady Anthea asked. Honestly, I had forgotten she was standing there.

"No," I said.

"No," John, that was his name, said at the same time. He smiled. "Go ahead. I'd love to hear your theory."

"Really?" A real live police chief wanted to hear my theory?

"Uh, no. Not really. But please, be my guest."

I sighed. "His work shirt is probably covered in blood and holes from the stabbing," I said. "I doubt the killer put that on. And he, or she, definitely wouldn't drive the van wearing it."

"The forensics team can tell me if they find fibers from it in the wounds. And I'll look at the camera footage later tonight. If someone else drove your van to the ferry, it suggests the rumor isn't true. And could be a big break in the case." He grinned then said, "Hmm, isn't there an old song about having that kind of luck?"

I did a double take at that last bit. "There is! It's 'All Shook Up'!" He was still being sarcastic as hell, but I loved that song. There was hope for this guy. "You're an Elvis fan?"

He chuckled. "Uh, no. I am not in the Elvis army." With that, he walked back into the restaurant.

I leaned closer to Lady Anthea. "Is there no end to that guy's smart mouth?" Turner stopped walking, but he didn't turn around. His shoulders bobbed up and down. He was laughing, so I knew he could hear me. "We're on the same team," I said. "I have some very nervous pet parents. I'm afraid they won't show up for the gala on Friday night...."

"Or that the unpleasantness will cause them to take their business elsewhere," Lady Anthea added.

At that, Chief Turner turned back to face us and our eyes met. We had had the same reaction to her referring to the ending of a life as unpleasantness.

But that's not what he spoke about next. "Why do you use that term, pet parent?"

Did I really want to get into that with him? I wasn't up to any more eye rolling, so I just shrugged my shoulders. Besides I had just seen someone come in the front door that I wanted to talk to. "Good night," I said.

I motioned for Lady Anthea to follow me and walked away. "Henry left Buckingham's with four dogs. The pet parent whose dog Henry dropped off just came in," I whispered to her. We pushed past the three-deep crush at the bar and made our way to the front door. "Dayle, this is my friend Lady Anthea Fitzwalter. We were just about to have dinner. Can you join us?"

She hesitated then nodded. "I would enjoy that, but I doubt I'll be very good company. I'm pretty beat." I wouldn't have said it for the world, but she did look pretty wrung out. She was wearing a baseball cap with the LSD logo, Lower Slower Delaware, not her usual stylish self.

We snaked our way through the crowd to the hostess stand. "Long day?" I asked.

"Yeah," Dayle answered, looking at the floor.

"Want to eat outside?"

They both did and the hostess accommodated us, seating us at a table on the deck and leaving us with menus.

I told Lady Anthea that many of the pet photographs at Buckingham's had been taken by Dayle. There wasn't much my partner could say since this was her first visit and I had dragged her out almost as soon as she walked in.

"I look forward to a more detailed look at all of them," Anthea said diplomatically. Wow, there's something to be said for this good breeding business.

Speaking of business, it was time to get down to it. It was just a matter of time before Dayle was on Captain Turner's radar. I leaned in. "You heard what happened to Henry Cannon?"

"No."

"Then you may be the only one in town who hasn't," I said.

Lady Anthea gave a snort, which was just this side of unladylike. "You know how rumors start around here. Anyway, the fact of the matter is that he was killed this afternoon some time after bringing Dottie home." The waitress had come to take our drink order. That was convenient because Dayle seemed to need a moment to get used to the idea that she was the last person, except the killer, of course, to see Henry alive. I almost forgot that I was at Gilligan's, not at On the Rocks, and ordered an Orange Crush, but caught the error in time to order a glass of Chardonnay.

"How did he seem when he dropped Dottie off?" I asked.

"Fine." Her left hand had flown to her lips and stayed there so she spoke through her fingers. One of those body language experts could probably say what that meant, if anything, but to me it looked like she might be sick.

Anthea put a reassuring hand on Dayle's arm. "Dear?"

"I'm okay. This is quite a shock. Do you mind if I don't stay for dinner?"

"Do you need a ride home?" Anthea asked.

"He didn't seem nervous or ...?" I asked.

"I can walk. My house is just a couple of blocks away. The night air will feel good." She was getting up to leave, but stopped. "He was fine, just his normal self."

She was off her stool, but Peter Collins was walking by and blocking her escape. "Oh, Peter," she said to him. "I got your phone message. I'm sorry I haven't had a minute to call you back. Can I telephone you in the morning?"

"No need. Everything's been taken care of," he said and walked on.

We waved goodbye to Dayle and watched her make her way back through the restaurant.

"Well, at least we found out Henry's state of mind just before his murder," Anthea said.

The waitress was back with our wine and took our food order. I ordered a crab cake—which you cannot go wrong with in Delaware.

"I'll have the same." I didn't know if she really wanted that to eat, or if it was for expediency.

"Dayle said she'd had a long day, and she looked it. Don't you wonder what a short day would look like if being home before five o'clock constituted a long one?" I mused.

"Hmmm." She took a sip of her wine, then studied the glass. I noticed she'd almost emptied it. Finally, she looked up. "If it's not too personal, may I ask if you've ever been married?"

"No, I've never been married."

"You're certainly attractive, so you must have had offers."

"Yeah, I guess I've had my share of marriage proposals. How about you? Are you married?" I asked.

"I'm widowed. I was married to my soul mate." Then she changed the subject back to me. "I enjoyed hearing your friends teasing you about being very picky about who you'll date. Have you just never met the right person?" I guessed even an upper-class Brit would ask personal questions if you mixed jet lag with wine drunk too quickly in the summertime night air.

How much did I want to say? We were business partners and all our communications had been Pet Palace-related. "I've seen how cruel people can be to one another. How things can start out so right, and go so wrong. No thank you. I would rather be on my own."

Something over my shoulder caught her eye, but she looked down right away. "Here comes the police chief. The young constable is right behind him."

"What's a young constable? Do you mean Wayne?"

She nodded.

John Turner sat down, uninvited. Wayne took the chair Dayle had freed up. Chief Turner was empty-handed, but Wayne had switched from beer to a mixed drink. Whatever happened to police officers eating donuts?

"Ms. Patrick. Lady Anthea." The chief gave us each a nod.

We nodded back.

"We'll be reconstructing the victim's day. This business about taking dogs to their homes—do all the dogs get a ride home?"

"No, just when the owner requests it," I answered.

"And pays a chunk of change," Wayne interjected.

"Had he made any of his…?" John searched for a word. "Deliveries?" He hadn't taken his eyes off me.

"Yes, one," I said.

"Where was that?" His tone was very *and where were you on the evening of blah, blah, blah.*

I thought about how Dayle had looked drained and tired and not herself. I couldn't sic this new police chief on her until she got some rest. "I'll have to look at my records at the office," I said. "I can do that in the morning."

"It was Dayle, the pet photographer, with the dalmatian named Dottie," Lady Anthea said. "We were just talking to her, but she left."

Turner swiveled his head and scrutinized me, one eyebrow raised in disapproval. This sent my mind into cleanup-on-aisle-seven mode, but I was too worn out to think of a clever rejoinder that would say, *this woman is not a justice obstructer.* The look on Wayne's face told me he was laughing on the inside.

I pinched the bridge of my nose and squeezed my eyes shut and thought about how a thousand years of upper-class British reserve had just succumbed to a cold glass of a fairly good Chardonnay. "Looks like she has a better memory than I do," I said.

Lady Anthea looked at Wayne, by far the more approachable of the two men. "You're from a different agency than he?" she asked. Both men nodded. "Is that why he's in uniform, and"—she hesitated here, taking in his outfit—"you're not?"

"No, ma'am." Wayne's big hand wrapped around his glass, dwarfing it, and he lifted it to toast her. "I'm dressed like this because at this hour, I take my orders from Captain Morgan."

Chapter 4

It was just shy of seven in the morning when Lady Anthea walked into my office. "Sorry to be late. I wish you had knocked me up."

"You know that expression means something completely different for us, right?"

"In the U.K. it refers to getting someone out of bed, but in the States it involves getting someone into bed." She had made a joke, not the greatest but enough so for me to do a double take. She looked proud of herself. Her smug expression made me laugh.

"I just thought you'd want to have, I believe you call it, a lie-in."

"Oh, no. I was looking forward to observing your start-of-day procedures."

"Why?" It wasn't the first time I'd wondered about her interest in the least interesting aspects of the pet resort. After all, she was here for the week to give us some royal street cred thereby validating our business theme. That was her part of the bargain. Mine was to be in at six o'clock, six thirty on the days I jogged on the beach, and work until seven o'clock or later every night, seven days a week. "I mean, there's really not a lot to see. I like to spend a few minutes catching up with the overnight staffers. Then I go over my calendar for the day to see if there are swim lessons or agility lessons I have to give."

"How many employees are here at night?"

"Usually two, but sometimes three, depending on how many boarders we have." I stood. "We didn't have time for our tour yesterday. Would you like that now? Shelby is handling the reception desk."

"But that's not what you were doing this morning, was it?"

"No. Have a seat." I carried the tablet I'd spent the last half hour on to the white leather sofa. "Let's sit over here."

She picked up the throw pillow, embroidered with an Elvis impersonator bloodhound, and moved it to the side.

"This is Henry's tablet. It's the one we issued him and he'd left it here. He should have had it with him, and I don't know why he didn't. Anyway, the password is one we set, so I know what it is. I've been going through his emails. The police will probably want this and, before I give it up, I want to see if there are any work-related emails. Like special requests or anything about future pickups that haven't been transferred to our main files."

"Are you sure you weren't trying to find information that might lead to your employee's killer, and stay one step ahead of Chief Turner?"

"Maybeeee."

"Let the professionals do their job. Don't draw attention to what happened," she said.

"Aren't you suspicious about how most of the town knew about Henry's death so quickly?" I asked.

"I remember people from that outdoor pub looking on," she countered.

"That's On the Rocks, and that's a stretch to think someone drinking there would call Charles Andrews. Besides, it's on the other side of the building." Several of the waitresses were my friends, and I already couldn't wait to tell them that our local *no shirt, no shoes, no problem* hangout was an outdoor pub. They'd love it. "Anyway, look what I've found. This came in yesterday morning." I read an email to her. "*Sorry, Henry. My bad. You need a sign saying if this van's rockin', don't come knockin'. Right?*"

"What does that mean?" She hadn't taken her eyes from the screen. Though I could only see her profile, I could tell she was as serious as a Chihuahua staring down a blow-dryer.

Where to start? "If a van is rocking, there might be a couple inside having sex."

"Henry could not have been snogging in the van here in Delaware last weekend. His fiancée said she hasn't seen him for the last month."

"You're kidding, right?"

She started laughing. Thank the Lord. Another joke. What her comedic skills lacked in quality she was determined to make up for in quantity.

"Obviously, I didn't know him as well as I thought I did. This email is from Rick Ziegler. Some of our dogs are on raw food diets, and he's our supplier. He's about Henry's age, late-twenties, early-thirties, something like that. Henry picked up our orders in the middle of the day and that's how they knew each other. I thought you and I could go today and ask a few questions. We can leave right after the morning rush."

"What morning rush?" Shelby was standing in the doorway.

I was always half listening to the lobby in case I needed to help out. Now I listened with both ears and heard nothing. It was quiet. Lady Anthea and I followed Shelby out to an empty lobby. "The campers have all been checked in?"

"We had twelve cancellations," she answered.

I took a deep breath. "The grooming appointments start at eight. No cancellations there, right?"

"Five cancellations. There would have been more if I hadn't talked them into home visits," Mason called from the hallway.

He and our second groomer were running toward us in the lobby dressed like the Beatles, pointed-toe boots and tightly fitted suits. Actually they weren't running; their ultra-skinny pants wouldn't let them. Mason slowed when he saw Lady Anthea and bowed. Joey, who Mason called his wingman, did the same, and they were gone. Sort of a reverse British invasion.

"Thanks, guys!" I yelled after them.

"Love you!" Shelby blew them kisses.

"Uh-h-h." Lady Anthea seemed at a loss, but recovered nicely. "Carry on!" she called out.

The elevator door opened and two part-time employees came out, laughing and talking. They stopped short when they saw Lady Anthea. They had yet to meet her in person. She was dressed in a similar style as yesterday. She wore an expensive, well-cut skirt and blouse.

Lady Anthea stepped forward and introduced herself. "Good morning. Was it a long evening?"

"No, ma'am," they said in unison.

I had stopped by last night to check in on them. I was proud of their loyalty and poise and came around the counter to give them each a hug. "We have six moms who job-share the night nanny positions."

The taller of the two, Taylor Dalton, said, "We work when our husbands are home and that saves us from paying for childcare."

Lady Anthea clapped her hands. "Brilliant!"

She beamed and I had to laugh at her reaction. Sure, it was a win-win solution to a staffing need, but she sounded like we'd won the lottery.

"But, ladies, isn't working through the night difficult?"

"We're moms. We're not used to sleeping!" said Laurie Williams. "And it's just a couple of nights a week." She looked at her watch. "Gotta scoot to be home before the day camp bus comes."

After they left I turned to Shelby. "All our employees showed up, right?"

"Every single one of them." A ring that sounded like a bicycle bell came from the computer at the reception desk. Shelby extricated her glasses from her hair and put them on. Then she began clicking away on the keypad. I joined her behind the counter. "We have a Google alert set up to notify us when we're mentioned on the internet, like when someone posts a Yelp review," I explained to Lady Anthea.

"Oh, yes. I'm aware of them. We do the same for mention of Frithsden or one of our charities or, uh, friends in the press," she said.

A *Southern Delaware Daily* article loaded onto the screen. The first words I saw were *Murdered Employee*. I looked out at the empty lobby. "I can't breathe."

Shelby put her hand on my arm. "This is just the online edition. We don't know how many people have seen it."

"From this empty lobby, I'd say lots of people have read it," I said.

Anthea joined us and we stood on either side of Shelby and read the article. It was bad. There was a grainy photo of the van taken from a distance some yards away. I read the headline, "Murdered Employee Found in Buckingham Pet Palace van." The barking dogs were described as traumatized. The article byline was Staff Writer. Whoever that was had repeated the rumor that the dogs were about to be taken out of state, via the ferry. Scrolling down, there was a photo of Lady Anthea and me standing next to the van. Chief Turner was looking at me. He was quoted as saying he had not notified the next of kin, so could not make the victim's identity public.

Shelby leaned closer to the screen, almost touching it. "So that's the new chief of police? I want to get me a piece of that."

"Hey, girl. I think Jeffrey might have something to say about that." I stopped staring at the newspaper photo long enough to say to Lady Anthea, "Jeffrey is her husband." I had read enough. "So we know Chief Turner spoke to the press. You still trust him not to be the source of that rumor?"

Lady Anthea turned from the screen to face me. "He *is* the proper person to handle a...." Here she wrinkled her nose and lifted her chin. "A murder inquiry."

I shook my head. "Does that mean you don't want to go with me to pick up the dog food and talk to Rick Ziegler?"

"You're determined to interview him?"

"*Interview* might be putting too fine a point on it. I'm going to ask him about the email." I turned to Shelby, who was restocking the supply of tip envelopes. "Did you know Henry was engaged?"

"He was?" Shelby raised her eyebrows in astonishment.

"Seems so. His fiancée lives in Albany," I said.

"He never mentioned her." She shook her head.

"Do you know who he hung out with? Any friends?"

I must have drawn out that last word. This time it was just one eyebrow shooting up. "And cheat on himself? Nope, no fri-e-n-ds that I know of. He always gave the impression that we, the dogs, and the pet parents all bored him stiff." The decision to fire Henry over his poor customer service skills had been a joint one between Shelby and me. "It's weird that he never told us about his family. I guess what we took to be aloofness was actually him hiding his secrets."

"But why would he lie about being engaged?" I asked. "I mean, of all the things to lie about that's an odd choice."

"Indeed," Lady Anthea said.

Shelby shrugged and went back to the article, clucking now and again.

***

I gave Anthea her promised facilities tour, then she said she wanted to stroll around the neighborhood. We agreed that I'd work on payroll until nine o'clock when we'd leave for the ten-mile drive to Milton—not to be confused with other nearby towns of Milford or Millsburg.

When we got to Raw-k & Roll, Rick Ziegler was hard at work behind a heavy oak country kitchen table. He was spooning the raw dog food into plastic bowls. His gloved hands flew, but he had a meditative expression on his face. I had to raise my voice to get his attention over a Ziggy Marley tune coming from a speaker I couldn't see and the whine of the two meat grinders along with an industrial size food processor. "Hellooooo." He looked up and then did a double take at Lady Anthea in her tan skirt and white silk blouse. He took her in from her pearl necklace to her sensible heels. Someone this formally dressed was definitely a first for his establishment.

I followed his gaze. She was examining Rick's full but well-ordered workshop. Freezers and refrigerators lined two walls. Wicker laundry baskets and wooden crates of fresh fruits and veggies sat on immaculate mismatched tables. There were too many to count. "Are you okay?" I asked her.

"I think I know how Howard Carter and Lord Carnarvon felt."

"Huh?" Rick asked. His long, black ponytail hung from his HLFM baseball cap. This time of year a lot of his produce comes from our Saturday farmers' market. It's real name is the Historic Lewes Farmers Market.

"I think they discovered King Tut's tomb," I said.

Rick smiled. "Cool. Beer?" He held out a bottle of Dogfish Head Summer Ale. The brewery's motto is "Off-centered brews for off-centered people."

I knew Rick a little from surfing and that pretty much described him too. His drinking philosophy was unique. He says you should be sober for the best part of your day—which is after work hours. That's why he was drinking beer at 9:45 in the morning. I could make out the whir of at least three pieces of machinery he was operating, what you might call a chink in the logic of his thinking.

I make a point of never saying, "A little early for me," when offered a beer in the morning because I don't want to be judgmental. So I just smiled and shook my head.

Rick held the beer toward Lady Anthea, who simply stared at it. I'd like to think it was out of a desire not to be censorious, but honestly, it was probably surprise.

I held up my bag of Raw-k & Roll BPA-free containers from the last batch that Henry had cleaned out before he left to drop off the dogs yesterday. "Put these over here?" I motioned to an open spot in the corner of the room.

"Nah, just throw them in the sink. They get sterilized before we reuse them. I'm working on your order now. Almost done." He reached over a basket of mixed organic vegetables and flipped the off switch for the grass-fed beef grinder and then the other machine which was processing hormone-free chicken. The food processor had timed-out and shut itself off.

Lady Anthea leaned closer to me and whispered, "This must be costly. Are all the dogs fed this food?"

"Lord, no. Just the clients who pay for it." I mouthed, "Let's talk about it later." I didn't want to be disrespectful of Rick's religion. Actually, it was getting caught that I minded, since Rick was a legend for pet parents who worship at the church of raw food.

"Did you hear what happened to Henry Cannon?" I asked.

"Since you're here to pick up the order, I'm assuming you canned him." He dropped a heavy spoonful of meat into a container and pushed the lid onto it.

Even though that was exactly what I had intended to do, I resented the implication that I was trigger happy. I told Rick the whole sorry business, as far as I knew it.

He picked up the next plastic bowl, then put it down again still empty. "Man." He shook his head side to side. "Who would've done something like that?"

"I want to know the same thing. Since this happened, I've been feeling like I didn't know Henry at all. But you seemed to have."

"Yeah, I guess."

"Who were his other friends?"

He shrugged his shoulders and hesitated, about to turn a machine back on. I helped him along. "I saw your email to him. Did he have a lady-friend who he would take out in the Buckingham van?"

He chuckled. "Take out?" Then I realized the laugh meant he would not have expressed what Henry was doing in the van exactly the way I had.

"How about for a hook up?" As I live and breathe, this was from Lady Anthea.

My head jerked around. Rick's head swiveled to her. He seemed as shocked as I was to hear those words from such a proper Englishwoman.

"Well?" she asked.

He nodded and grinned sheepishly.

"Who was it?" I asked.

"Couldn't see."

"Then how do you know it was a woman he was with?" Lady Anthea asked.

Rick looked down at the table then he mumbled something that sounded like, "I just figured—uh, ya know."

"But you know Henry was in the van?" I asked. "You saw him?"

"Nah, I heard him."

"What was he saying?" I pressed on, but it was slow going.

"I couldn't make out any words, but I got the general idea."

"Where was this?" I asked.

"At sunset on Lewes beach with the old pe—.... No offense."

"None taken." I wasn't offended because I was probably only five or so years older than him, but significantly more grown up.

"They were watching the sunset?" Anthea asked.

"Uh, they were in the van at Lewes Beach. Let's just leave it at that," he answered.

"And this was night before last?" I asked, just to be sure. Since he had emailed Henry on Monday, I assumed he had been referring to Sunday night.

Rick furrowed his forehead and looked at the ceiling. "Depends. What's today?"

"Tuesday."

He seemed to be taking the question up with an advisory council in his head. "That would make yesterday Monday. Yeah, I saw the van Sunday night."

Then he made a mistake. I caught him looking longingly at his assembly line on the countertop. If he wanted to get back to work filling his precious containers that badly, he could tell us what we wanted to know instead of making us wrest every word out of him. I mentally put myself sitting on my surfboard at Cape Henlopen with gentle waves rocking under me, lifting me up then lowering me. I smiled at Rick, with the knowledge that I could wait all day.

He took a deep breath. "I know it was a woman because Henry had talked about meeting someone. He used to brag that they were getting together almost every night. I only saw him the one time since I tend to go to beaches that are off the beaten path, instead of Lewes Beach, but I believe what he said." At long last.

I slapped my insulated tote bag on the counter. He loaded my order and insisted on taking it to the Jeep for us. I knew when I was being escorted out and left gracefully. Lady Anthea, however, was not going quietly.

It was her turn to prod him. "May I ask one last question, Mr. Ziegler?"

"Sure." As if he had a choice.

"Why did you assume Mr. Cannon had been dismissed when you saw that we were picking up the order today?"

Rick looked at me. "She never met Henry, did she?"

I shook my head. *Not when he was alive* was what I wanted to say, but I held myself back.

"Henry was lazy and dishonest, and often bragged, which doesn't go down well in a small town. I try to get along with everybody, especially good customers, but he was not—I think you would say—a mate. That's why I figured he'd been fired."

"Thank you for your forthrightness. We'll be on our way," she said and got in the car for the drive back to Buckingham's.

Almost before the end of Raw-k & Roll's driveway, Anthea said, "So we learned that Henry had a lover."

"Still wonder why I've never gotten married?" I asked.

"I was married to the most wonderful man in the world for almost twenty years. He died three years ago and I miss him every day." Her voice was so soft that if we'd been riding with the top off the Jeep, I wouldn't have been able to hear her.

"I'm sorry."

"Let's talk about what we learned from our interview that wasn't an interview," Lady Anthea said.

"I learned that Henry was using the van outside of work hours. Hmm. Too bad we didn't find out who he was with. Why don't we go to Lewes Beach tonight and ask some of the regulars if they saw the van there at sunset? Maybe someone there will know who he was with," I suggested.

When we pulled into the side driveway of Buckingham's, who did we see but Chief John Turner.

"Ms. Patrick." He touched the brim of his hat. "Lady Anthea." Ditto with the hat touching. "I have some news."

I could feel Lady Anthea looking at me. I hadn't decided if I was going to tell him about the email and the mystery woman, or our plan to ask around at the beach.

"Henry's cell phone was found on Cape Henlopen Drive near the ferry entrance. A jogger found it and turned it in to lost and found. This is one law-abiding town you've got here." Except for the murder. We let that part go unsaid. "It was probably tossed from the van."

"So that tells you which direction the van was driving from?" I asked.

For some reason, this made Turner smile. "Not necessarily. The killer could have tossed it on the way to or from the ferry terminal. There's more. The phone had been wiped clean." He paused and I was pretty sure it was a test to see if I could figure out what that meant.

"So he was killed by someone he knew? Because he wouldn't have called or been called by a stranger?"

That got me a nod and a slow smile, which ended somewhere up behind his Ray-Ban aviator sunglasses. And it got me to show him mine.

"We have an approximate time of death. He was killed around four thirty in the afternoon," he said. "And the stabbing took place inside your van."

I didn't have a response to this. It made the murder too real.

"Fibers from his uniform shirt were in the wound," he continued.

"So he was wearing it when he was attacked?" I asked. The fact might mean something to a law enforcement person, but meant nada to me.

Chief Turner nodded but didn't say anything.

Lady Anthea reached out her hands for the tote bag. "I'll take the food in, to get it refrigerated," she said. I handed it over, and she smiled at me.

While we had been standing there, a few employees and clients had walked by, and I'd spoken to everyone I saw. After this morning's cancellations, I needed all the good will I could get. When the area was clear of people again, I went ahead and told him about the email from Rick Ziegler on the tablet Henry used and our visit to Raw-k & Roll, figuring two out of three wasn't bad.

"So Henry had a girlfriend on the side." He lifted his hat and ran his hand over his head. "Ms. Trent says she never visited him here. I'll ask again this afternoon when she gets to town, just to be sure it wasn't her in the van."

By some unspoken consent, we were walking toward the front door of Buckingham's. "I, uh-h…" he began.

"You need the tablet? I'll go get it for you."

"Thank you." The gentleness in that baritone voice took me by surprise. "Hey, when are you going to tell me why you call dog owners, pet parents?"

"Right after we opened, we received an email from someone who objected to the term dog owner. She said 'you're a guardian of a pet so the ethics are different from owning property.' She made a good case, so we began using the term pet parent. We're not trying to say dogs and children are equal, but the decision to bring an animal into your home should be carefully thought out."

He smiled. "And I'm assuming it's called the Buckingham Pet Palace because of Lady Anthea?"

"Nah, it's because Heartbreak Hotel was taken."

"Very funny," he said. "You know, I have a feeling if Ziegler knew who the affair was with, he would have told you. You have that effect on people."

"Yeah, well, I'm going to need every bit of my charm after that *Southern Delaware Daily* article," I said. Thoughts about the future of my business weren't far from my mind.

"You know that rumor about the dogs being taken somewhere didn't come from me or the department, right?"

"At first I thought it had, but now I don't. The article said he drove the van to the ferry parking lot and, thanks to me, you know he didn't."

I turned a little too quickly and saw a confused look on his face. Then he grinned and pointed to the windows on either side of the door—where two women were high-tailing it back to the reception desk.

Inside the two sets of double doors, Abby was barking and pacing, anxious to greet me. After I rubbed her back, she turned to Chief Turner and looked up at him. He was looking around the lobby, taking in the large photograph of Lady Anthea. Abby was unaccustomed to being ignored and had no intention of getting used to it. She pressed her head against his leg.

"This is Abby," I said.

He looked down at her and moved away.

"Have you changed your mind about letting me be there when you question Ashley Trent?" I asked.

"Not even a little. Absolutely not."

Chapter 5

Though all the home pickups had been cancelled, there was still plenty of work to do. I kept myself busy sanitizing the inside of the mini-indoor-cabanas dogs go into for their afternoon naps. Unfortunately, very few would be needed today. To my surprise, Lady Anthea pulled on a pair of rubber gloves and helped me.

At noon the two of us, along with Shelby, took a break to have a sandwich at my desk. As soon as I sat down, my phone rang.

"Do you mind if we tuck into ours?" Lady Anthea asked, picking up her ham and Swiss.

I mouthed, "go ahead," and answered the call.

"Ms. Patrick, this is Chief Turner. I'm trying to interview someone who brought her dog with her. The dog is distracting and I'm finding it difficult to—"

He was interrupted by a women's high-pitched voice in the background. "He's just sitting here, not bothering anybody."

"She says it was too hot for her to leave the dog in her automobile. Can the dog stay at Buckingham's for a short while?" It was cute that he still couldn't bring himself to say *Pet Palace*, but he'd come around eventually.

I put him on speaker phone. "Not even a little," I replied. "Absolutely not." I let that lean on him a few seconds before giving him an out. "Maybe we could make a deal."

"I'm listening."

"It's Henry's wife-to-be you're trying to question, right?"

"Correct." Chief Turner was wound up even tighter than usual. That's not healthy and it's very un-Lewes like.

"I can't have her dog here at the *Pet Palace*,'" I said, emphasizing our correct name for his benefit. "I don't have his vaccination records, and we haven't completed a behavioral assessment to be sure he's not aggressive and that he can get along with other dogs. I am, however, happy to offer a dog walker who can come and exercise him while we conduct the interview." "Just a second." I heard a chair scrape along the floor and then a door being opened. "While *we* conduct the interview?"

Had I gone too far?

He continued, "I will conduct the interview and you can wait in the viewing room. You'll be able to hear and see everything."

"Lady Anthea and I will be there in five minutes."

She had finished her sandwich and was sitting on the sofa going over personnel files. "Another Ride of the Valkyries?" she asked after I hung up.

I was pretty sure that was from something classical. When she dropped lines from poems or book titles into emails, I could google them, but what was I supposed to do now? It sounded vaguely familiar so I lobbed a guess. "That's an opera?"

She nodded and closed the folder she'd been reading.

"Is there an opera about a police chief who's afraid of dogs and armed?" I asked.

***

The police station was in the Lewes City Hall Building on East Third Street, and we were there in no time. Chief Turner was waiting outside for us and walked up to me on the driver's side of the Jeep. "Park over there," he said, pointing to a reserved space at the end of the block.

In the summer, parking is at a premium, so I was doing a happy dance with a feather boa in my head at his words. I parked, and we walked back to meet him in front of the one-story red brick building with its robin's egg-blue shutters. Lady Anthea's cell phone rang, and she took it out of her shoulder bag. She took one look at the screen and frowned.

"I'm afraid I need to take this," she said and walked a few paces back the way we'd come.

"So Chief Turner, where is this dog?" I asked.

"It's in the lobby." He looked around me to Lady Anthea. "Will she be able to handle this dog by herself? It looks like something's wrong with it. Like, he's not normal."

I stopped walking. "How so?"

"His tongue is mostly blue. It's a little black, but mostly blue."

"And he's big?"

"Extremely. She says he just has a lot of fur. His name is Lion King. That should tell you what he's like."

Lady Anthea walked up. "I apologize for delaying you."

"It's fine," I assured her. I told her the dog's name and that he was a Chow Chow, a beautiful breed despite Chief Turner's accurate, if not exactly flattering, portrayal. She gave us a curt nod, and we marched inside to make his acquaintance.

Ashley Trent was perched on the edge of a sofa and at her feet sat a well-behaved long-haired dog. She stood as we approached. Long, straight black hair framed her young face. *Forlorn* is a word we don't hear very often, but it accurately described her. She appeared lost. Her dark eyes darted between the three of us.

"I'm Sue Patrick and this is Lady Anthea Fitzwalter," I said. "We're so sorry for your loss." I held out my hand to shake hers, and she looked at it before taking it.

"I'm Ashley Trent. You worked with Henry, didn't you?"

Out of the corner of my eye I saw my co-owner's eyebrows shoot up at the *worked with* reference. I'm as egalitarian as the next boss, so it hadn't really bothered me at the time.

"I'll be taking Lion King for a walk," Lady Anthea said, reaching for the brown leather leash. Ashley sat back down, still clutching it, and seemed to be considering whether or not to relinquish it.

I sat next to her on the couch. "I understand how much comfort and security our pets are to us when we're in pain," I said. "It's like they know we need them, and they're there for us, sometimes in a more meaningful and authentic way than a person can be."

Ms. Trent looked down at the dog, and I was afraid I had made her cry. You could have heard the proverbial pin drop. Then she handed Anthea the leash.

We watched the two of them walk out into the sunny day.

Chief Turner looked at me. "Wait here." Then to Ashley Trent. "Let's go back to the interview room." On their way down the hall that spoked off the lobby, he motioned to a young female uniformed officer and she filed in behind them. Turner opened the door for the two of them to go into a room midway down the hall, then returned to me. "I'll show you to the observation room."

To call the space he led me into a room would be unfair to rooms in general. It was an opening between two real rooms and usually reserved for wiring and insulation. The width was the same as the door we had entered. I'm not usually claustrophobic, but it was dark in there and I was going to be left alone. The thought made me wish I had Abby there to reassure me, the way Lion King had bolstered Ashley Trent. Suddenly I felt Chief Turner's arm reach around my back. "Whatha...?"

"I need to open this curtain. And you're facing the wrong way. You'll need to turn around if you want to see anything."

He pulled a cord and once I turned around, I could see into the stark interrogation room where Ashley Trent sat at a wooden table, across from the police officer.

I turned to Turner. "You couldn't talk to her in an office? You're treating her like a suspect."

"The discovery of the other woman makes her a person of interest," he whispered.

"She wasn't even in town when he was murdered."

"You're probably right. Even if she'd flown, instead of driving, she couldn't have made it back to upstate New York when I talked to her. I reached her on her cell phone, and we placed her in a suburb of Albany. I do love technology." He leaned against the back wall and crossed his arms.

"Don't you have some place to be?" I asked and pointed to the large window. "I think it's inconsiderate of you to make her wait. Her husband-to-be was murdered yesterday and it's obvious she's grieving. Why can't you be kind to her? This is a small town, and we don't treat people like that when they're down."

He straightened and said, "You're right." Then he took a side step and was out the door. In a matter of seconds I saw him go into the room where Ashley Trent and the uniformed police officer waited.

He started by apologizing to her for the delay. "You said earlier that Mr. Cannon relocated here about three months ago?"

She nodded in agreement.

"Did he ever mention anyone that he did not get along with, or that he had argued with? Anyone that might have a grudge against him?" Turner asked.

"No! Everybody liked Henry. He's, uh, *was* that kind of guy." Ashley didn't sound defensive. She sounded like a loyal woman in love.

"So, you can't think of anyone from either here or from before he moved here that might want to harm your fiancé?" He was pursuing this line like a dog with a bone.

She shook her head. "Who would want to kill the CFO of a pet spa?"

Chief Turner reached around to the other officer and held out his hand for a manila folder she had brought into the room. He opened it and rifled through the first few pages. "He worked as a Chief Financial Officer at a pet spa in Albany?" He had paced the words so there was no mistaking what he was asking, though I wondered why. It hadn't been an obtuse question. I didn't remember it from his resume, but it wasn't a hard question.

"No, here in Lewes, Delaware." She looked across the table at him with a *you're not very far along with this, are you?* expression. "Henry was the CFO of Buckingham Pet Palace." She hesitated and studied her hands. "I hope they're going to be okay without him."

There was just enough room where I was to let my mouth fall open. At that point, I didn't want Abby with me; I wanted Shelby to hear this. She would really get a kick out of that. At least if I fainted, I wouldn't fall, there wasn't enough room.

"Weeeelll," Chief Turner said. "They'll have to worry about that, won't they?"

"He came home once a month. It was hard on us, but we've been able to get ahead financially."

So far the chief hadn't trusted himself to look up from the file, but his head shot up at this mention of money. "He had extra money?"

"Oh, yes. He had never made a six-figure salary before. Though I don't know why. Henry was one of the smartest people I've ever known." Ms. Trent teared up and Chief Turner pushed the tissue box at the end of the table her way.

I made a mental note: *Set up audit with accountant.* Just as soon as I could breathe again, that's what I'd do. I was frozen in place. Almost everything the business made went back into it. A nice surfboard, a car that runs, and new running shoes when the old pair wears out was all I needed. I had a lot of friends and I had the Atlantic Ocean. Why be greedy? Though I pretty much lived on subsistence wages, I paid Shelby, Dana, Mason, and Lady Anthea as much as I could. None of us pulled down six figures. They made very real contributions to Buckingham's. Henry hadn't.

That was when I realized Chief Turner and Ashley Trent were talking. I guess he had asked her a follow-up question about the money, like had she seen a bank statement? There was hope. Maybe Henry had just *told* her he made a lot of money. That had to be it. And that would be just like Henry to brag. I was beginning to breathe again.

"Of course. I pay the bills. His base salary isn't that much, but with last month's bonus check we were able to get out of debt. We bought a new car, and we were planning a cruise for our honeymoon. Our wedding was supposed to be next spring," she said. She trailed off at the last. "We've been living together for almost three years."

"I'm sorry you're seeing Lewes for the first time under these circumstances, Ms. Trent," Chief Turner said. He sat silently after that, and I'm pretty sure just pretending to look at the folder. She didn't take advantage of the dead air to contradict him.

As far as I was concerned, she hadn't been to Lewes before and she wasn't the woman in the van. After all, why would she lie about visiting the man she was about to marry? Whether or not it would satisfy Chief Turner was another matter. He didn't believe people for a living.

And he wasn't done. He closed the file and leaned forward. "Had the deceased made friends here?"

I whispered into the dark, "Please don't go there." Surely he wasn't going to tell this grieving woman that the man she loved had been unfaithful to her. Why inflict this extra bit of cruelty when all he had was what Rick, a not exactly stellar witness, *hadn't* seen? I liked Rick. To a certain extent, we're kindred spirits, but he's definitely an acquired taste.

"Oh, no. Ms. Patrick makes her staff work a-l-l-l-l the time," Ashley said. "Once I called Henry pretty late at night and she had him at the beach walking a dog. Can you believe that?" She shook her head at the harsh conditions Henry had had to bear up under.

It was hard to tell whether or not John was still listening to her. He had turned to the mirrored window. He was looking at me and I was looking at him, but we weren't seeing each other. Finally, he returned his attention to the desk and closed the file. "I'm sure you want to get started making arrangements." I thought about how each major life event has its own assortment of euphemisms.

"Chief Turner, until I have to plan his funeral, I can still tell myself that this isn't really happening."

He nodded then picked up where he left off explaining the next steps in the process of having Henry's body released.

I slipped out of the confines of my cupboard and headed for daylight as fast as I could.

Chapter 6

I found Lady Anthea sitting on a bench in Canalfront Park, facing the water with Lion King, regal and attentive, at her feet. The park was built in 2006 and includes twenty-two dock slips plus a launch area for canoes and kayaks. A step closer and I saw she was slumped over the dog. I took off like a greyhound, running up behind her. When I got near them, I saw she was leaning into the dog's mane, and her lips were moving. I slowed down to catch my breath. She was talking to him in a low voice, almost a whisper.

"I am so tired," she said to the dog, who twisted his head and nuzzled her face. "Servants?" she said in response to the dog's imagined inquiry in their tête-à-tête. "Not in years. We occasionally hire someone from town to work on the grounds and once a week a service comes in to clean the part of the house we can still occupy." She patted the dog's back and pulled him in again to huddle. "We would have enough money to repair the house if my brother—he's the duke, you know—would listen to reason. He makes a hash of everything he touches. I wish he had one tenth the business acumen of Sue Patrick. So many of the historic country homes are used for weddings and corporate gatherings. There's no shame in it, but all he cares about is the family name. The money I make from my partnership here in the States with the Pet Palace has kept the house from falling down around our ears. Not to mention saving the family's art collection."

She had financial trouble? How could someone with a title, living in a house with a name, have money problems? That explained her all-in attitude toward the business. Shelby, Mason, Dana, and I had been grateful for the use of her name and the photos. Her input and involvement were gravy. This new info also explained why she had chosen my spare room to stay in over the Inn at Canal Square. I almost said, "Ah-h-h," out loud.

I had no right listening to this. My nosy evil side was scuffling with my better nature, and it was only a matter of time before they'd come to blows. It was perfectly okay, expected even, to eavesdrop on strangers, but not on friends. And that's what Lady Anthea was now. It would take all the strength I had, but I needed to speak up and let her know I was there. She continued, "That was him calling to tell me—"

To tell her what? Did I really have to do the right thing right then? "Uh, Lady Anthea, Chief Turner has finished talking to Henry's fiancée." She lifted her head from the Chow Chow's furry neck. I could see she was, just as she'd said, tired. As soon as she registered that I was there, she gave Lion King a quick pat and raised herself to a Jacqueline Kennedy level of fortitude. "Who is Ruth Africa?" she asked, motioning for me to join her on the bench.

Before I could answer, I felt I needed to take her emotional temperature. "Are you okay with everything that's happening here?"

She smiled shyly. "This is the most excitement I've had in years."

I sat next to her. "Ruth Africa? I think she's involved with the Harbor of Refuge Lighthouse preservation. Does she have something to do with the case?"

"No, but this bench is dedicated to her so she must be famous." She pointed to the four-inch commemorative inscription on the back of the bench.

"Uh, it doesn't work like that here," I said, hoping she'd let it go. Putting your name on a bench, a paving stone, a wall, anything immobile was the preferred way for charities to raise money in Lewes. I always advise tourists against standing in the same spot for too long lest they get themselves labeled. "I wanted to tell you what Ashley Trent said in her statement."

"Did she incriminate herself? Has the case been solved?"

I hated to burst her bubble. "No confession, sorry to say." When I was three-quarters through telling her about Henry inflating his job title and salary, I heard someone calling my name. It was Chief Turner.

"Sue, where did you go?" he asked, keeping a wary eye on Lion King.

"I would have thought it obvious that I've come to the Ruth Africa bench."

"Huh?"

"Never mind," I said. "I was telling Lady Anthea what Ashley Trent said about Henry." I turned to her. "We'll have our accountant go over our books."

"I'll get the victim's bank records," John said.

"He came into all that money last month, the second month of his employment, if that helps narrow it down," I said.

He nodded then rubbed his hand over his head. "Could you tell if she knew the victim was having an affair?"

"I didn't get that sense." Did he think women could read each other's minds? Lady Anthea stood and, unfortunately for John, the dog did too. "Oh, Chief Turner! You can't possibly think that slip of a girl could overpower Henry and stab him." She looked at me and chuckled. "Perhaps if she coshed him first."

"If coshed means feeding him enough sleeping pills to drop an elephant, sure," he said.

Lady Anthea sniffed. "Someone is forgetting their P.G. Wodehouse." Chief Turner stopped his staring contest with Lion King long enough to glance my way for a translation.

"Don't worry about it. He's a British writer. A cosh is like a club you hit someone over the head with," I said, drawing the insight from my recent read of *The Fishmonger's Cod Cosh*. The book had not been a favorite among reviewers, partly owing to the title revealing the answer to the mystery. It had been an unorthodox but interesting choice by the publisher.

Chief Turner looked back at the dog. "Cosh, huh? I wish I had one on me now."

"Be serious. Are you saying Henry was drugged?" I asked.

"Yeah, with run-of-the-mill prescription sleeping pills."

I turned and looked at the lazy, plodding water in the canal, so unlike the ocean. There were thousands of salt-tolerant plants in the park, but it was the water that interested me. "Chief Turner, the pills weren't his, were they?" Then I answered my own question. "We know he didn't take them voluntarily, since he would hardly overdose then wake up and stab himself."

He shook his head and a slow smile started on the left side of his mouth. "There were no medicine bottles in his home."

"The sleeping pills belonged to the murderer," Lady Anthea ventured.

"Maybe. Probably," Chief Turner said. "The toxicology report showed them in his system. He had a water bottle in the car and that's where we found the residue."

"Dare we hope for fingerprints on the bottle?" Lady Anthea asked.

"Only Mr. Cannon's. His killer was wearing gloves."

"Might that show a degree of professionalism?" she asked. There was a degree of eagerness in her tone that I understood. A contract killing by an Asian gang of money-laundering sex traffickers was more appealing than the idea of one of our neighbors being a murderer. This stain that had come upon our community would be removed if that was the case. Trouble was, it didn't fit reality any better than the dogs-being-smuggled-to-Canada fantasy.

Chief Turner shook his head. "Anybody who watches TV knows to wear gloves when committing a crime." He reached his right arm over his left shoulder and tried to knead away a knot of tension. "I've sent someone to talk to the pharmacists in the area."

"Did you sleep last night?" I asked.

"I got in a couple of hours," he said.

"Can you tell when the sleeping pills were put in the water bottle?" I asked. The chief shook his head, no. "Doesn't really matter. We know he was stabbed in the late afternoon. That's the important time frame."

"There's my good boy!" Ashley Trent and a female police officer were headed our way.

If either Lion King or his mom thought the dog was going to be freed to run to her, they would have to think again.

"Stay!" Lady Anthea's voice was low but strong. Yelling at a dog is rarely, maybe never, needed. She had looped the leash around her hand and given him very little slack. Had it been around her wrist, instead of her palm, the dog could have pulled her to the ground. Then she calmly walked the dog toward Ashley.

That left Chief Turner with me.

"I had better get to work on those banking records."

"Yeah, I hear those people keep strict hours," I said.

He started to walk off and then stopped. "Thanks for, uh, you know." He pointed to Lion King. "I appreciate it."

"You're welcome. Did you find anything interesting on Henry's tablet?" I asked.

"No comment. I don't appreciate your dog-sitting that much."

"So you still don't know who the girlfriend was?" I whispered.

He looked at Ashley and then shook his head, no.

"Did you talk to Henry's last pet parent yesterday, Dayle Thomas?"

"Yeah, she said he dropped her dog off just before five and left. Everything was normal."

"Thank you for not telling Ashley about the other woman just yet," I said. He was leaning over me so I could keep my voice low enough not to be overheard.

Then for some reason he straightened up, turned on his heel, and walked away. As he passed the three women with Lion King, he motioned for his officer to accompany him. Lady Anthea, Ashley, and the dog joined me.

"Ashley, where are you staying?" I asked.

"I— I don't know. I just grabbed a few things and jumped in the car when I got the call," she stammered.

"The Red Mill Inn on Route 1 headed north, allows dogs. The owner's a friend of mine. I think you'd be comfortable there." I pulled my phone from the side pocket of my shorts and scrolled for the number.

Ashley had her phone out and ready to key in the number. "Thank you."

"Is Lion King up-to-date on his vaccinations?" I asked. In my peripheral vision I could see Lady Anthea's eyes widen. She was wondering where I was going with this.

"Yes," Ashley said, "including one for kennel cough."

"Every Wednesday morning we take some of the daycare dogs swimming in the ocean at Dewey Beach. Want to bring Lion King?"

"He loves to swim," she said. She leaned over to pet him again, not that she'd taken her hands off him since they reunited.

"We meet at seven o'clock. I think the exercise will do him good and make up for his time confined to the hotel room," I said.

"Thanks. I'll call that hotel now." She sat on the bench we'd vacated to call the hotel.

Lady Anthea moved around so her back was to Ashley and the dog. "You just want to be sure we see her again in case we have more questions, don't you?"

"Oh, yeah. What if that money was coming from Buckingham's?"

She nodded in agreement and we turned back to Ashley.

"They have a vacancy. We can go there now," she said.

"Brilliant," Lady Anthea said.

After we said our goodbyes, Ashley and Lion King headed for the municipal parking lot. Lady Anthea and I were walking back to the Jeep when I stopped and turned. "Ashley, wait." I caught up with them and gave her my cell number. "Call me if you need anything or if you just need to talk." By that I meant any secrets she wanted to unburden herself of.

Chapter 7

On the drive back to Buckingham's my phone rang. The screen on my dash said the caller was Mark Lizzi and under that was the name of a local radio station. "I'll let it go to voice mail," I whispered to Lady Anthea. After absolute decades of this technology, I still couldn't shake that feeling that the caller knew when I was there but pretending not to be. "I bet he read the *Southern Delaware Daily* article. He probably wants a statement."

"You're not going to let them interview you, are you?" Lady Anthea asked.

"No way." I was nowhere near as nonchalant about the media request as I hoped I sounded. I pounded the steering wheel with both palms and pulled into the parking lot of Beebe Medical Center. "I just remembered something. This is the station that promised to broadcast live from the gala. Maybe that's what he wants to talk about."

To my surprise she said, "We need to stay in their good graces."

I reached for the call-back button on the screen, but before I took the plunge I looked over at Lady Anthea. She nodded and gave me a thumbs-up. Simultaneously hoping the reporter would answer and praying he wouldn't, I pressed the green button. He answered before the first ring finished.

"This is Sue Patrick."

"Yeah?" he growled.

"From the Buckingham Pet Palace? You just called me?"

"Oh, yeah." The guy had a true mastery of the English language. "I was looking for a statement about what occurred last night."

I didn't know if he was referring to the attempted dog theft rumor or about Henry's murder. Then I realized it didn't matter. My answer was the same for either. All the books I'd devoured and the episodes of *Masterpiece Mysteries* I'd watched had prepared me for a moment like this. "I can't comment on the *ongoing* investigation. We were saddened by Mr. Cannon's death and our thoughts are with his family."

The reporter was asking me what I assumed was a follow-up question but I wasn't listening. Lady Anthea was pantomiming a message for me. She saluted and then pressed her wrists together in her lap.

"I'm sorry, you're breaking up," I lied to the reporter.

Then Lady Anthea looked up at the sky and batted her eyelashes, grinning. I had it.

"The Lewes police are working hard to find his killer. Lady Anthea and I have complete trust in them." With what little strength I had left, I thanked him and said goodbye.

"How was that?" I asked as I collapsed back into my car seat.

"Brilliant! We need to stay in the good graces with the police too."

She was laughing, but I hadn't forgotten about her comment about being tired. "Should I drop you off at home for a nap?"

"I'm fine. We'll have to drive the dogs that get door-to-door service home, won't we? I'll help you with that."

We were back at Buckingham's in minutes. The lobby was empty except for Shelby. In addition to missing pet parents, we were missing an employee. "Where's Dana?" I asked.

"She's taking the day off."

"She didn't want to come in? Is she upset about Henry?" I asked, disappointed, but also concerned.

"It was her mother who didn't want her to come in today," Shelby said, looking down.

"The murder of someone you worked with is a lot for anyone to take in. I guess it's worse for a young person." I looked around. I quickly told her about what Ashley Trent had said about Henry's title and salary. By the time I got to the point in the story about him being drugged, she was propping herself up against the counter in shock. "Lady Anthea and I were going to take the day camp dogs home in the Jeep, obviously since we don't have our van, but I can drive by myself and she can stay here with you."

"Actually," Shelby said, drawing the word out, "there's no one to drive home."

There hadn't been any dogs to pick up this morning, but I'd been holding out hope for half-day campers, or for the pet parents who drop the dogs off themselves and have us deliver them home. Nada. "How does the schedule for tomorrow look?"

"Sorry," Shelby said. "We have about half the number of usual reservations."

"Tomorrow is Wednesday. What about So-Long?" I asked. I turned to Lady Anthea. "He's the dachshund we took home last night."

She nodded that she remembered him. "His owner, Mr. Andrews, seems to think the dog's blood sugar levels warrant your special attention."

"That's the one," Shelby answered. "Mr. Andrews doesn't drive and So-Long comes in every Monday, Wednesday, and Friday. But not tomorrow. I got a call from him about an hour ago. He said that So-Long was traumatized and that this was a time for families to be together."

"He's a widower. Does he have children in the area?" I needed to sit so I went behind the desk and plopped down on a stool.

"He meant So-Long's family. Remember So-Long's father, So-Lo, who rarely comes to day camp because he's fifteen years old? That's who he was talking about."

"Are we in freefall?" I asked the two of them and the empty room in general.

Shelby answered first. "Everyone will come back as soon as the murder is solved."

I got up and started pacing back and forth behind the reception desk. "But what if it's not solved this week and we host a very expensive gala for ourselves? It will be an embarrassment, and I don't know if the business can recover from it."

"Dr. Walton would absolutely love that," Shelby said. She took her glasses off and rubbed both eyes. That's how abhorrent the image was to her.

"He's the veterinarian who lost boarding clients to us?" Lady Anthea asked. She was standing in the same spot and stock-still except for the swiveling head.

"Yup," I said. "He would love to see us fall flat on our faces."

"Or on our something else's," Shelby said.

"There's only one thing to do," Lady Anthea said, straightening herself taller.

"Let's do it!" I yelled. "Let's find the murderer."

Lady Anthea's mouth formed an O in shock and she blinked. Once she recovered, she held up her hand in a stop signal. From the look on her face the gesture meant the same thing in British English that it does in American English. "Excuse me. I'm afraid I'm gobsmacked." She walked into our store area and then back to Shelby and me at the reception desk. "Solve the murder ourselves?" she asked in disbelief. "I wouldn't know how to begin."

"We'll start by retracing Henry's steps," I said. "Dayle Thomas told us and Chief Turner that Henry seemed fine when he dropped Dottie off, so I guess that means he hadn't been drugged at that point."

Lady Anthea rubbed her forehead. "Sue, I got the impression you thought she knew more than she was saying."

"She didn't seem herself. The Dayle I know would have talked to half the people in Gilligan's last night. She's a one-woman Chamber of Commerce for Lewes. And she certainly wouldn't get home at five o'clock and call it a long day." I scanned the calendar on Shelby's computer screen. "We're obviously not needed here. Let's pay her a visit."

"Before you go," Shelby said, "Lady Anthea, what were you about to suggest?"

Our favorite Brit shrugged her shoulders.

I knew what Shelby was talking about. "You said that there was only one thing to do," I reminded her.

"I was going to offer to give an interview to your newspaper to refute the rumor about Henry trying to steal the dogs, but that seems a little tame now." She laughed. "And we need to be at your Lewes beach at sunset to see if anyone saw who Henry was with in the van."

She was in.

"Quand le vin est tire, il faut le boire," she said.

"Can't argue with that," I said. "No idea what it means."

"When the wine is drawn, it must be drunk," Lady Anthea said.

Shelby tilted her head. "Of course, it must. It's wine. But what does that have to do with catching a killer when you don't know what you're doing."

"It's the same as 'in for a penny, in for a pound,'" Lady Anthea said.

That we understood.

Chapter 8

Dayle's Victorian home was one block off Second Avenue on a quiet, tree-lined lane. Lady Anthea and I hadn't parked in a driveway because there wasn't one. We walked from the street up the path made of crushed seashells and river rock, flanked by lush hybrid rose bushes alternating white and ruby-red. Hydrangeas stood guard before the wraparound porch.

Lady Anthea pointed to a wooden projection from the house. "What's that?"

"It's an outdoor shower. They're convenient for washing the sand off after a walk on the beach, before you go inside."

She cocked her head in disbelief and only started to walk again once she was sure I wasn't pulling her leg.

I knocked on the screen door and tried to think about how to start this conversation.

Dottie ran to the door and stood wagging the rear half of her body, animating her spots.

"Who is it?" Dayle called from somewhere in the house.

"It's Sue Patrick and Lady Anthea Fitzwalter."

"Come on in. The door's not locked."

The wood floor was covered in paper, which was covered with construction dust. White sheets were draped over the furniture, filling the rooms we could see into with ghostly blobs.

Dayle descended the stairway which divided the floor in half. "Sorry, I have to use the bathroom up there." She pointed back up the way she'd come. "What a mess! And it was worse, if you can believe that. I told the contractor I needed to take a break. I wanted a week with no noise or dust. Isn't redecorating just so much fun? LOL. Ugh."

I was happy to see a spark of her old vivacity. The Dayle I knew was in there somewhere. Dottie was pressing against her knee, and she gave the dog a pat on the head.

I tended not to stay in any one place long enough to redecorate so I couldn't sympathize with her domestic problems. "What are you having done?" I asked.

"The upstairs will become my home office and two studios, and I'll live and entertain down here." She hesitated and scanned her living room, like she was looking for something and not finding it. "Can we go into the kitchen?" Without waiting for an answer, she turned and walked down a short hallway to the left of the stairs.

"You know I'm photographing two-legged animals now, right? Not just pets," she said as we walked.

"Yeah, I heard that," I answered. "Why are you expanding? Don't you get plenty of bookings?"

"Yes, but as an artist, I'm always looking for something new to try. My work often includes owners, or as you say, pet parents, along with their dog or cat so this isn't too much of a departure."

When we got to the kitchen, Dayle lunged for the farmhouse table and sagged against it. Startled, I grabbed her waist before she fell and supported her. She felt light as a bird. Lady Anthea pulled a chair out and I helped Dayle lower herself onto it. I bent over her and rubbed her back.

She looked down and then propped her elbows on the table and covered her eyes. "Thanks," she said and gave a half-hearted laugh. The effort of putting on a good show had exhausted her. "I think I'm losing it. I let myself run out of sleeping pills. I thought I had enough to last the week." She looked up at me and then Lady Anthea and sighed. "Anyway, no sleep for me last night."

Lady Anthea handed her a glass of water. It had been done in such an unobtrusive way and was such a kind gesture that I was ashamed of myself for how picky I, and everyone I knew, had become about what kind of water we absolutely had to have. This was a glass of tap water offered unbidden and gently by a stranger.

"Thank you," Dayle and I said at the same time.

I took in her thin, limp hair. "Chemo?" I asked.

She nodded. "Please, please don't tell anybody."

Lady Anthea and I took chairs on either side of her. I spoke first. "Of course not. I'm so sorry you have to go through this."

"I think I know why you're here, so let me make it easy for you." She gave me a weak smile and took a sip of water. "I have a confession to make."

Noooo, I thought. She couldn't possibly have murdered Henry. Could she? "At Gilligan's you asked me how Henry seemed when he brought Dottie home. The truth is, I wasn't here when he dropped her off," she said, looking at me and then Lady Anthea. "I'm sorry I lied to you, but I haven't told very many people about my diagnosis. I just need to deal with this in my own way, and I won't be able to if everyone around me sees me as a patient." Her voice had gotten stronger as she spoke. "Dammit, I'm still me!"

The emotion was so raw it brought tears to my eyes. "I'm so proud to know you." It was all I could say.

"I was getting a treatment, but I didn't want to say that. Sue, I lied to the police too. What are they going to do to me?"

"Absolutely nothing." Lady Anthea said this with a certainty only people born into her privileged world have.

As for me, I wasn't so sure. I was thinking about a police chief looking for a suspect. Henry had been poisoned with sleeping pills, and I was ready to put money on them being Dayle's. Thank goodness she had one whopper of an alibi. "So you didn't see Henry on Monday?" I asked.

She shook her head. "I knew he had been here since Dottie was in the house."

The dog was waiting just inside the kitchen door and heard her name. The young Dalmatian dog scrambled to her feet and came to get herself some loving from her mama.

Dayle reached her arm out to her. "Weren't you, girl?"

Lady Anthea took this opportunity to give me a furtive look. "Does everyone in Lewes leave their doors unlocked? Yours wasn't locked today."

"I don't know many people around here that *do* lock their doors—in the daytime, at least," Dayle answered. "Henry knows, uh, knew," she corrected herself, "that I leave the door unlocked for him if I go out. That way, if a shoot runs long, he can let Dottie in." She smiled at the Dalmatian. "She plays so hard the days she has day camp, she conks out when she gets home."

"Did you read the article about the murder in the online edition of the paper this morning?" I asked. It was time to see if I could count on her for the gala, since there was nothing she could tell us about Henry's last hours.

"About Henry stealing the dogs? That's crazy. Most of the time I am here when he drops Dottie off, and he always seemed like he couldn't wait to get rid of her." She ran a hand over Dottie's floppy ear, just in case the dog had heard what she said.

"I apologize," I said, because the buck always stopped with me. "He was too lazy to plot anything like that, wasn't he? I know I shouldn't talk like that about the dead."

Dayle shrugged as if to say that didn't bother her in the least.

Lady Anthea got up. "Dear, we should go. You do look knackered, if you don't mind my saying so. I hope you'll sleep better tonight."

"If you happen to hear anybody else talking about the scheme, would you please tell them it wasn't true?" I got up and gave Dottie a goodbye pat. "Will we see you at the gala Friday night?"

She looked at the glass of water. "Just try to keep me away." She gave the Lazy Susan in the middle of the table a nudge and it rotated clockwise a few inches bringing a cluster of prescription pill bottles within reach. She picked up one and shook it. "But tonight I will sleep!"

Chapter 9

"I suppose Henry's memorial will be held in New York?" Lady Anthea asked on the drive to Lewes beach. Next on our investigation to-do list was to try to learn the identity of Henry's lover. Back at Buckingham's I'd worked at my desk until close to sunset. Since Delaware is "home to tax-free shopping," I have less paperwork than business owners in other states, but at the end of each month I certainly had enough to cut into my surfing hours. My accountant had called back to report that my business bank account balance was what we thought it was. Henry had extra money from some place, but thankfully, not Buckingham's. Shelby, Lady Anthea, and I had been so relieved at that bit of information we'd deputized a part-timer and celebrated with frozen yogurt from the SnoYo around the corner.

"I guess so. Why do you ask?"

"Too bad. In a number of the crime dramas, the murderer attends and stands off to the side of the real mourners. If that happened in real life, we could identify the killer while staying out of harm's way," she said.

"Sure thing," I agreed with a laugh. "Oh, well. I don't go to funerals."

"Never?"

"Ever," I answered. "Or weddings."

"Why in the world not?" Lady Anthea asked, sounding very interested.

"At funerals, people lie about the past. At weddings, they lie about the future. I just don't want to be a part of it."

"But isn't that the pact we make with people that inhabit the world with us? That we'll participate in these rituals together?" she asked.

"Yeah, I guess," I said. "I don't know…" I let the sentence drift off. I'd shared a lot, maybe over-shared. The truth was that when I was younger I'd tried— I'd really tried—to join in, but… Then we were at Lewes beach and I didn't have to finish that thought.

I pulled into the parking space next to a late model Lexus occupied by a middle-aged couple licking ice cream cones. Their windows were down which made them easy pickings for my questioning. I approached the man in the driver's seat.

"Hi. I'm Sue Patrick and this is Lady Anthea Fitzwalter. We're the owners of the Buckingham Pet Palace," I said.

"Oh, yeah. We don't have a dog right now, but I see your place when I go across Route 1," came his friendly answer.

His wife leaned over. "We're sorry to hear about your loss." She stopped here to give me the opportunity to fill in any gaps or share any juicy tidbits on Henry's murder.

"It was quite a shock—"

I was interrupted by a British voice over my shoulder. "What we need to know is if you saw our van here at sunset? And who was with Henry? Because he was—"

"Easy there!" This time I was doing the interrupting and not a second too soon. It hadn't been my intention to ask that in so many words. She had made it sound like the Honda van was lost and we needed their help finding it. We were there to quell a rumor, not kick the Lewes rumor mill into overdrive. I turned back to the couple in the car. "You're here to relax and we wouldn't want to spoil it." His wife looked like she would like nothing better. "But, have you seen the Buckingham van parked here at sunset?" I wanted to get the information on who was with Henry in the van without anyone wondering: one, why we wanted to know and two, if I had lost all control over my business. I couldn't come up with a convincing way to dial back what Lady Anthea had started, at least not on such short notice.

He squinted, thinking. "No," he said.

She shook her head. "Sorry, no."

I pulled an invitation out of the pocket of my shorts. "Even though you don't have a pet, I'd like to invite you to the gala this Friday."

They took the invitation and thanked me.

Next I led Lady Anthea to a white SUV that had pulled up on the other side of my Jeep. Thankfully, she let me take the lead. I introduced her and then I assured the fifty-something gentleman that it was business as usual at Buckingham's. I had no reason to think he had been concerned, but hey, if he regularly saw the van at the beach, he might be. I paused. He shrugged and the gesture told me all I needed to know. He hadn't noticed the van there.

We repeated the act with car after car, speaking with people there to walk the beach, and those arriving to sit and watch the sunset.

Two couples walked up to one of the white wooden benches and sat. All four wore shorts and tank tops. We walked up as the young women were pressing their toes into the warm sand. "Ahhh," they said. I recognized one of the women who worked at the day spa at the Villages at Five Points.

"Janice, right?" Even out of context, I recognized her because of her long, thick strawberry-blond hair.

"Yeah, hi!"

"Best feeling in the world, right?" I asked, kicking off my sandals. I picked them up and noticed Lady Anthea looking at our five pairs of bare feet. She glanced at her expensive leather pumps. She didn't make a move to join us. Her upper-class feet would remain imprisoned.

I introduced Lady Anthea, and Janice introduced the other woman as Kathy and said she was a facialist. Kathy offered Lady Anthea a complimentary treatment, and I gave out invitations to the gala.

Janice introduced us to the guys, both had bulging biceps and pectorals. James, I think his name was, had tattoos running the length of each arm. I had noticed in the last year or so this trend of inking from shoulder to wrist, referred to as sleeves. Then I asked if any of them remembered seeing our van parked there at Lewes beach. No luck. All four shook their heads.

We said our goodbyes, and Lady Anthea and I started walking back to the Jeep. I happened to glance back, and all four of the people on the bench had turned to the left to see what progress the sun was making going down. The two women had their heads on their guy's chests, and the men had their heads tilted over their date's heads.

I pulled out my cell phone to call Buckingham's to ask Shelby to walk Abby and take her home. While I updated her on our lack of progress, my eyes wandered over the paved parking lot dotted with cars, wondering if there was anyone else who might have seen the van who we could ask.

Shelby sighed. "What would Elvis do?"

Lady Anthea was still watching the backs of the heads of the foursome. At the same time Shelby was asking her prescient question, Anthea said, "True love," and sighed too.

I looked at my phone, to Lady Anthea, then to the couples on the bench. I guess I'd been living right because an idea clicked in my head. Something wasn't right. True love. What would Elvis do? "Shelby," I said, "I'll call you back." There was a light, sugary coating of sand on the asphalt. Something wasn't right. Along with these thoughts I had an Elvis song in my head, something about true love. "True Love Travels On A Gravel Road." That was it, that was the title of the song.

"Look at this parking lot," I said.

Lady Anthea looked up and down the line of cars. "It's just a car park."

"There's no gravel here."

"I don't understand."

"Let's go!" I sprinted the rest of the way to the Jeep.

"I'm right behind you," she yelled at my back.

I jumped in and reached over and opened her door.

"Last night I saw the police pulling gravel out of the van's tires and bagging it. The Lewes Beach parking lot is paved with asphalt, not gravel! Buckle up."

"Where are we headed?" she called out as I swung out onto Savannah Road on two wheels.

"Roosevelt Inlet! We have to get there before the sun goes down, or there won't be anyone for us to talk to!"

Chapter 10

After a short but, at this time of year, slow drive along Cedar Street, we passed the Lewes Yacht Club, then dead-ended at the Roosevelt Inlet parking lot. My tires crunched over the gravel, and I smiled at Lady Anthea like a deacon holding four aces. She laughed and then her eye landed on something over my shoulder. To our left and over the bridge was the four-hundred-foot-tall wind turbine.

I said, "That was a joint project of the University of Delaware and the Gamesa Corporation. No one minds if you refer to it as a windmill, since that's what it looks like, but technically it's a turbine. It was erected in 2010."

"It's tremendous," she said.

I nodded in agreement. "Each of its three blades is one hundred and forty feet long." I pointed straight ahead on the opposite shore. "That's a Coast Guard installation." Then I pointed to our right, out to sea. "Beyond the inlet is the Delaware Bay and then the Atlantic Ocean."

"This is all just so interesting," she said. "The English coast is quite varied, but no part that I've visited is like this."

We got out of the Jeep and I continued my commentary. "You haven't seen anything yet. When you're on a boat, you can tell when you've left the bay with your eyes shut. The temperature drops and the water gets choppy."

Two people were seated on folding chairs on the little rocky bit of land at the end of the parking lot, in the direction I'd pointed. The man waved at me and I saw it was Garrett Coleman. He was with his wife, Pam.

That was as good a place as any to start.

"Hi," I said. Garrett was pushing up from his chair, but I told him not to get up. I leaned over to hug him and then Pam. Then I introduced Lady Anthea.

Garrett reached out his hand to shake hers. This time she extended hers without missing a beat, and without overdoing it. Then he looked up at me. "Sue, I'm sorry to hear about Henry."

"Thanks. You knew him?"

"Sure. We used to see him and Mary Jane Kerwin here all the time. Hard to believe we all stood right here several nights last week."

"We saw them Saturday, Garrett," Pam corrected. "Two nights before he was murdered."

Garrett considered what she said and nodded.

I nodded, too shocked at how the information had just fallen into our laps to trust myself to speak. We must have asked twenty people at Lewes Beach. Lady Anthea's mouth had dropped open. I didn't know what she was about to say and I didn't know what to do next, so I just kept nodding my head up and down like an idiot. Is a thank-you called for in a situation like this? Suddenly she snapped her jaw shut and gave me an uncertain smile. "The sunset!" she cried and pointed west across the waterway.

Garrett's, Pam's, and my head jerked that way. There it was: red and orange and round. Lady Anthea exhaled, proud of herself for the excellent save—two nights in a row.

It was time to drill down and find out if they had anything else to tell us. I went for a casual tone. "I met Mary Jane at Buckingham's but it's been a while."

"Mary Jane works at the Best of the Past," Pam said.

"The new antiques gallery on Second, right? The one owned by Peter Collins?"

"Yeah, that's the place," Pam answered.

"We met him last night at the pub," Lady Anthea told them.

"Gilligan's," I specified. "She brought her Saint Bernard puppy to puppy school," I said to Lady Anthea. I almost added "and I haven't seen the dog since," but stopped myself since I didn't know what Henry had told Garrett and Pam. Or what he had left out—like the part about being engaged to someone else.

They stood up and folded their chairs. "You're leaving?" I asked in surprise. For a split second it seemed like they were going because they'd already given me my answer, then I realized we could all leave since the sun had set.

"Yeah," Garrett said, giving me a quizzical look. "We leave as soon as the sun goes down. Mary Jane and Henry would sit with us, then we'd get in our car to go home and they'd sit in the van and talk awhile."

Since I was not blessed with a poker face, I dropped my head and looked down, going for a grieving look.

Garrett was talking again. "I hope Mary Jane is okay. What a thing to happen. Have they caught whoever murdered him?"

"No, but they're working on it. You know the rumor about Henry trying to steal the dogs was just nonsense, right?" I asked, looking up.

Pam laughed out loud. "Oh, yeah. Henry couldn't wait to get away from dogs at the end of the day. The stories he used to tell. He cracked us up."

"Like what?" I asked.

"All the crazy things dog owners would ask you to do," she answered. "Like the dogs on raw food diets. Puh-leeze. Or grain-free snacks. He said he didn't know how you listened to them with a straight face."

Their chairs were folded, and so we said goodbye and they headed to their Volvo. Lady Anthea expected me to follow them, but I was rooted to the spot. "I kept a *straight face* because I respect our customers," I said to her.

"And you care for the animals," Lady Anthea said. "I can tell that. The whole town can." She pointed to a group of three people walking along the path that ran from the back of the yacht club to the beach.

I had been vaguely aware of a deep voice on the breeze and now I saw it was Chief Turner. He was accompanied by the mayor and his wife. Swell. Just what I needed. I jerked my head back to Lady Anthea, hoping Chief Turner hadn't caught me looking at them.

"Let's get out of here," I whispered. On one hand, I wanted to know if he had learned anything from the camera footage at the entrance gates to the ferry parking lot; on the other, I didn't want to tell him about Mary Jane Kerwin since we were conducting parallel investigations, so to speak, on the identity of Henry's Lewes girlfriend. But then I also wanted to know if they had found any fingerprints in the van.

Lady Anthea interrupted my thoughts. "You want to leave because you can't decide whether or not to lie to him?"

No one could accuse her of being a flatterer, but she was right. "You read my mind."

Chapter 11

We chose On the Rocks at the ferry terminal for dinner, where we could eat outside and Abby could join us. I'd taken the top off the Jeep and we were using beach breeze air conditioning as we sped along Kings Highway. Elvis was singing at the top of his lungs. I twisted around to Abby, harnessed in the back seat and sang a few lines to her.

Suddenly Lady Anthea screamed, and I lurched back to the way I should have been facing all along. A car with headlights on high beam had wandered over into our lane. I tried to shield my eyes from the glare with one hand while I drove onto the verge of the road and came to a stop. The other driver corrected and got back into his lane and flew past us. "That was close! Are you okay?" I put a hand on her arm.

Lady Anthea was looking in her side mirror. "He's turning around." She reached for her door handle. "I'm going to give him a piece of my mind!"

I checked my rearview mirror. He was closing the gap between us at a high speed. An apology was definitely not what he had in mind. "Close your door!"

I pulled back onto the road and floored the accelerator. Since I was starting from zero, the other driver quickly caught up with me and was inches from my bumper. Would I be able to make it to the ferry parking lot and the DRBA police? Too bad I never had time to find out.

My reaction to the first bump from his car was to try to brake. I resisted the urge but it wasn't easy. Next he collided against the driver's side of the rear. I wanted to think that meant he was going to go around us, but when the third hit came, I knew his aim was to knock us off the road and down the embankment.

With the next strike, I lost control of the car. We were airborne from the force of the impact and because of the ground sloping steeply from the road. In those few seconds my eyes teared as I thought about not being able to protect Abby. At least I'd harnessed her into the seatbelt, even though it was just a short trip. Would the harness hold? It had never been tested before.

Honestly, when we hit the ground, the impact was not as bad as I thought it would be. The paved walking trail was straight ahead. On the other side was woods. If I could brake on the trail, we had a shot at avoiding hitting a tree—or several trees. Half thoughts raced through my mind. If I oversteered at this speed, the Jeep could flip. Just because we hadn't somersaulted when we were airborne, didn't mean we couldn't now. I turned the steering wheel to the right as sharp as I dared and I braked. We stopped. Both passenger side tires were on the walking trail. Not so for the driver's side, but the nearest tree was a good three or four inches away from my door. We were alive. I looked in the rearview mirror for Abby. With her dark coloring, I couldn't see her, but I heard her breathing.

"Pow!"

Then the world was white. Maybe we weren't alive after all.

"Bloody airbags!" Lady Anthea said, sputtering.

I turned to look for Abby and she was there. Then I could breathe again. She had the usual Schnauzer serious look on her face and waited for me to offer an explanation on this new game. "Hey, baby," I said.

I listened for the sound of someone running down the embankment. Say, maybe the driver of the car that had put us in this predicament. Just night noises from the woods and the canal.

"I'm afraid I owe you an apology," Lady Anthea said.

Of all the things she could have said at that moment, that may have been the last I would have expected. I had almost killed us. Then she continued. "For a moment I thought he was driving on the correct side of the road and you were wrong!"

"Apology accepted," I said. "Are you all right?"

"Never better, and you?"

"Other than being too close to this tree to get out of the car, I'm fine."

She batted the now limp airbag out of her way and looked out my side window. "I see what you mean. Just rest for a minute." She looked around the floor board. "If I can find my telephone, I'll call 9-9-9 to report the accident."

Her use of the British emergency telephone number told me she was more shaken than she was letting on. "Here, let me." I rearranged my flattened airbag so that I could press the screen and make the emergency call. I told them we were unhurt. We didn't need an ambulance but would need a tow truck.

"What was the make of the other car?" the dispatch operator asked.

"I don't know," I answered. I looked at Lady Anthea and she shook her head.

"The model?"

"We couldn't see it."

"The color?"

"Sorry."

"Did you see the driver that ran you off the road?"

"'fraid not."

She had our location from the signal and said help was on the way.

I unhooked my seatbelt. "If you can get out, I think I can climb over and get out on your side."

Lady Anthea looked at the console between the seats dubiously. "Better you than me." She opened her door and got out.

I scrambled over and got out of the car. I found I needed to lean on the Jeep before I could unhook Abby. "I'm afraid I'm a little unsteady on my feet," I confessed to Anthea.

"Just give yourself a minute," she said.

I took a deep breath and then reached in and released Abby's seatbelt. "Should we try to climb that?" I said, pointing up the steep embankment.

The end of my question was drowned out by a police siren. The sound had been getting closer, and I could see a red haze up the hill on the road. Then the car drove past us. After a few yards the noise stopped, but I could still see the pulsing light. Then I heard Chief Turner's voice. He identified himself, then asked someone, "Where did you say she was?"

Suddenly Abby leaped out of the car and took off up the hill. She was a blur of gray. "Abby!" I screamed. My strength came back and I took off after her. There was no way a driver would be able to see her in the dark. I reached the top and looked in both directions for her.

"What?!" Obviously she had startled Chief Turner. "Is your name, uh, Abby?" He hesitated. Though I doubt he would ever admit it, he was waiting for an answer from my girl. "Shoo. Go find her."

"Grab her collar," I yelled.

I looked back to check on Lady Anthea. She was still at the bottom of the hill, so I trusted him to do as I'd asked while I went back down to help her. Meanwhile, back at the road, Chief Turner tried to *shoo* Abby again. Obviously, she hadn't obeyed. And he didn't have hold of her collar.

"What an idiot. You can't *shoo* a Schnauzer," I whispered. I offered Lady Anthea my arm.

"I'll get a lead out of the car," she said. "Go ahead and get your dog."

"Are you sure?" I asked.

"Shoo!" she said and we laughed.

I took off back up the hill, yelling as I went. "Grab her collar!"

"No," was Turner's answer.

By that time I was close enough to the top of the hill to call Abby myself. She ran to me and I grabbed her collar. Not that hard to do.

"Are you all right? You're not hurt?" Chief Turner asked. I was kneeling by Abby and he came to stand on her other side.

"I'm fine. We're all fine."

He tried to look me in the eye; I guess to see if I was lying.

"According to the dispatch operator, you saw *nothing*?" After what I'd been through I could have done with a little less attitude from him. He pulled a notepad from his jacket pocket and started writing.

I told him about the large car veering into our lane and then making a k-turn to follow us.

"What kind of shape is your car in?"

Lady Anthea had joined me and hooked the leash into the ring of Abby's collar so that I could stand upright.

"Not a scratch on the bonnet," she said. "The driver's side and the back look unmarked, too, but that's all I could see in the dark."

"We'll just need help getting…"

I stopped when I heard an approaching vehicle and saw red lights. Turner turned on his heel and called over his shoulder. "Stop by the station for the accident report tomorrow. I've got something else to do."

"Thanks for nothing." My retort lost its entire sting because of the earsplitting siren. The EMT's got out of the Beebe Medical Center ambulance and approached us.

"Why are they here?" Lady Anthea asked me.

"Beats me, maybe it's standard procedure." I shrugged and went to talk to the man and woman.

"I'm afraid you've made a trip for nothing. Neither of us needs medical attention. Sorry, but I told the 9-1-1 operator that."

"He was the one that called it in." The older man jerked his thumb in the direction of the red taillights of the patrol car.

Chapter 12

By Wednesday, Buckingham Pet Palace was seriously short of both dogs and vehicles. We didn't know when we'd get the van back, but the Jeep should be road ready by the afternoon. Once the airbags were replaced, it would be drivable.

Shelby had already emailed and used all the social media tools at her disposal to get the word out that pet parents were to bring their dogs to Dewey Beach for the Wednesday morning dog swim, rather than to Buckingham's, and we hoped that at least a few of the six regulars would show up. Lady Anthea, Abby, and I were in Shelby's Prius driving south on Highway 1. Ashley Trent texted me to say she and Lion King would meet us there. Our first stop had been Starbucks. If Lady Anthea's accent didn't set her apart, her one-word order was certainly a first for the barista.

"I have an observation, or maybe it's actually more of a question," Anthea said when we got back in the car.

"Fire away."

"I hope this isn't offensive…" she trailed off. After a sip of her tea she began again. "Sometimes it seems Americans do things just because they can."

"That does sort of seem like a lot of us."

"For example, why would anyone add pumpkin to coffee? And why froth it after you've added milk?"

"I guess because we can."

For the next block or two she looked like she was pondering our eccentricities, then she said, "I think I could…" Her voice trailed off.

I waited for her to finish, but when it was obvious she wasn't going to say more, I decided it was time to bring up last night's accident that wasn't an accident.

"Do you think the driver knew—" I said.

At the same time, she said, "Do you think the driver—"

"Could we have been at the wrong place at the wrong time?" she asked.

"I don't know. At first, when he was in our lane and headed for us, I assumed he, or she—since, I never saw the driver's face—had fallen asleep and drifted over," I said.

"When he, *or she*, returned to the proper side and passed us, it was at such a high speed, the driver's face was a blur. I feel terrible that I wasn't more observant," Lady Anthea said.

"And it was dark. That didn't help. All I can state with certainty is that the car was large." We were stopped at the red light at Route 24 and I turned to her.

She nodded in agreement, her brow furrowed.

"When he turned around and chased us, I knew this was more than a random impaired driver. I think we have to assume it was personal," I said. "As if a murder on your first day in town wasn't bad enough, now I have to apologize for getting you into a second mess."

"What if this is one and the same *mess*, as you call it?"

Obviously she had never read *Long Rifle, Short Life*, nor come to think of it, *A Vodka Before Dying*. Of course, I wouldn't make her feel bad by pointing it out. "I believe killers only try to knock off amateur sleuths when they get close to solving the crime. Sure, we learned that Henry was cheating on Ashley, and yesterday we found out that it was with Mary Jane Kerwin, but that's all we do know. We're not a threat to anyone."

"We might learn more when we talk to Ms. Kerwin today," she said.

"Hopefully. Since she works most afternoons at the gallery, I thought we'd try to catch her at her house later this morning. What time is your interview with the *Southern Delaware Daily*?"

"They said they would stop by Buckingham's mid-day. They'll run the piece in their online edition." The way she kneaded her hands contradicted her casual tone.

"I'm sure publicity is abhorrent to you. I really appreciate this."

"You may have wondered why I didn't just get on the next airplane back to the U.K. after Henry's body was discovered. Perhaps I should explain."

"I accidently overheard you talking to Lion King," I admitted.

"Oh." She took a deep breath. "He was a very good listener. The truth is, not every historic home can be saved by a television program."

"Was Downton Abbey as popular in England as it was here?" I asked.

"Almost, but not quite." When she spoke again, it was to list the expenses for repairs at Frithsden, sometimes caused by an ancestor's neglect and sometimes just from the passing of time. She never mentioned her brother's mismanagement of the estate, showing admirable family loyalty. "So you see, the wellbeing of Buckingham Pet Palace is important to me too. More than I've let on."

We turned left onto Cullen Street at Fifer's Farm Market Café, and headed for the ocean, a mere two blocks away. I parked on the street, pulling in behind Ashley's new white Honda CRV. Lion King jumped out but stayed close by her side. Her eyes were puffy, and she quickly pulled on a pair of oversized sunglasses. If it was possible, she was smaller than yesterday. I felt a pang of guilt for leaving her all alone in a hotel room, but my guest room was occupied. Truth be told, even if Lady Anthea hadn't been using it, I would have lied about its availability. I doubted she'd killed her fiancé, but what if I was wrong? There was still the matter of Henry's infidelity. We had every intention of calling to check on her, but after what happened, I was in no mood to console anyone. We'd called Shelby to come over, and the three of us had drinks on my screened-in porch. I'd gone to bed filled with an unfamiliar anxiety. Before I drifted off I realized that I wanted someone to assure me that everything was going to be all right. That was all. I just wanted to hear someone say those words.

I helped Abby out of the car and she walked over to the bigger dog.

"It's a beautiful morning!" I said. "And it's almost low tide."

"Go ahead," Lady Anthea said to Abby, laughing. "Give him a head to bum sniffing."

This morning, she said she had slept well. I had owned up to feeling a little stiff from our fling down the embankment, but she had said she was well. Then why was she walking so slowly?

I was leading our group to the path that would take us to the beach when my cell phone rang. It was Chief Turner so I took the call and motioned for Lady Anthea and Ashley to go ahead. I handed Anthea Abby's leash, and they headed around the turn in the walkway made from weathered planks.

"Good morning," I said.

"It's a very good morning!" He was practically chirping.

"Uh, who are you?"

"It's John! Chief Turner," he said, a little deflated. I knew it was him but made a rule of not explaining sarcasm. You either got it on the first go-round or you didn't. "What did they say at the hospital last night?"

"We're both fine," I artfully assured him.

"You didn't go to the emergency room, did you?"

"If you knew we didn't go to Beebe, why did you ask?" I chose not to go because I felt fine and because I didn't want to, and I'd asked my

VIP guest if she wanted me to take her in to get checked out. She'd been adamant in her refusal. Her only caveat was something like, "Not unless you need a prescription for a gin and tonic in this country."

"Never mind. Look, I have news that I thought you'd be interested to hear. The fingerprint report on the van's steering wheel and door handle came back. As luck would have it, the prints matched someone in the system. Do you know a veterinarian named Dr. Raymond Walton?"

"Sure, his clinic is near Buckingham's."

"His prints were on file since he had a DUI last year. I can tell you that because it's a matter of public record." Not that I'd accused him of being careless with confidential information. "It gets better. I went to bring him in for questioning and what do I see but a dented fender on his Cadillac. I believe the paint in the dent is a match for the paint job on your Jeep."

I was glad he paused because this was a lot to take in. "So, he murdered Henry and ran me off the road last night?"

"He lawyered up immediately, so I haven't been able to interview him, but that is exactly how it looks to me."

I leaned up against the wooden railing. "Thank you," was all I could say. The nightmare was over. All of a sudden my business was safe. Lady Anthea and I were safe. She could pay her bills and I could have my life back. "Thank you," I repeated.

He laughed. "Everything's going to be all right."

I held my breath. He had said what I wanted to hear.

"Look, I'll call you back later. Walton's attorney just walked in. Looks like he brought an assistant with him." With that he hung up.

"Sue, you're going to want to see this," Lady Anthea called to me.

Dewey Beach was a wide, white, gleaming span. We were still "in season," and at night the crowd was young and loud, nothing like Lewes, but at seven in the morning dogs ruled. From the end of the path, I expected to see Kate Carter, Robber by her side, and maybe Dayle with Dottie. Instead, there was a large crowd of men and women and dogs mingling and running everywhere. Some bobbing in the ocean, some on shore barking at them. Dottie was already in the water, returning with a tennis ball. When they saw me, everyone turned to wave and shout. "Sue!"

I stared. "How many people are here?" I recognized Barb and Red and Jerry and Charlie.

"Must be thirty or forty," Ashley said.

I stood and looked out at the ocean. The tide was turning, and Abby and I ran to meet it.

Chapter 13

By the time I had played with the dogs in the soft sand and the surf for an hour, my thirty-eight-year-old body was feeling the full effects of the accident that wasn't an accident.

Anthea was somewhere in the crowd, working her public relations magic. Kate Carter had told the group about Lady Anthea's corgis having the same breeder as the queen's dogs, and at first that was all anyone wanted to hear about. Then she introduced Ashley Trent to the group. At first, I'd been uneasy because we didn't know if any of Mary Jane Kerwin's friends were here. What if they started discussing how she was holding up after her loss?

When they realized what a boon the forlorn, young Ashley could be to the Lewes rumor industry, the out-of-towner had all the company she could ever want. Now that play time was over, Ashley was walking behind me with Kate Carter. Lion King and Robber had fallen in love, or bonded, or something. As I huffed and puffed and led the group of pet parents and their dogs back up the hill, I saw someone standing on the path. The sea grass swayed in the breeze and I lost sight of the person. As I got closer, he walked forward. It was Chief Turner and his good mood was gone. I didn't care about his grimace. The murderer had been caught and, as this morning's turnout showed, Buckingham's was back and better than ever!

"I couldn't reach you on your cell so I called your business. Shelby told me you were here. Can I have a word?" His eyebrows were lowered and his lips formed a tight line.

"Sure," I said and reached down to grab my sandals. "Bye, everybody. See you Friday night at the gala!" I yelled to my customers. I motioned for Lady Anthea to join us, and we stayed at the entrance to the path and waited for the group to pass us by.

Chief Turner kept a wary eye on what can only be described as a procession of well-behaved dogs.

"Don't worry," I said, shaking my head at how constantly suspicious he was of dogs. "They're all worn out. All they want to do now is nap."

When Ashley Trent walked by, he nodded but didn't speak. He hadn't stopped her to give her the good news—a development she had every right to know. That was my first clue that something had gone wrong with the arrest. He stopped staring at the parade and turned to me. "We had to cut Dr. Walton loose," he said.

"You mean like until he goes to trial? Like out on bail?" He was scowling but I was smiling, holding onto my ignorance for all I was worth.

"I wish," he said. "Have you told anyone what I told you?"

"I told Lady Anthea that an arrest had been made," I said. When I had whispered to her that the killer had been caught, I told her we wouldn't need to visit Mary Jane Kerwin. And she'd been ecstatic that she wouldn't have to go through with the *Southern Delaware Daily* interview. "Not anyone else."

"I haven't told anyone," Lady Anthea said in response to my unasked question. "Isn't Dr. Walton the veterinarian? So that's who you arrested?" I hadn't given her a name, but she remembered our previous remarks about Raymond Walton.

"Yeah," he said. "The person that came with his attorney alibied him. She's a waitress at On the Rocks, and she swears he was at the bar for several hours up until the body was discovered, except for a short absence of about ten minutes around five o'clock."

Anthea grabbed at what she saw as a glimmer of hope. "It doesn't take long to stab someone! He could have murdered him in that time."

"I'm afraid not," I said, bursting her bubble. "Henry was killed earlier than that."

"Walton's absence from his bar stool was about an hour after the time of death," Chief Turner said.

I had been looking at the sand and turned to look up at him. "Wait a darn minute. What did you see on the security video?"

"Dr. Walton driving the van from the shoulder of the road into the turn lane for cars entering the ferry parking lot. That's what he said he was doing in the short time he was missing."

"Huh?" I said. "Why would he do that?"

"I beg your pardon, Chief," said Lady Anthea.

"The first version of his story was that he saw your van sitting along the side of the Cape Henlopen Drive with the engine running. He walked up to it and saw that there was no one in the driver's seat."

"How did he see the van? On the Rocks is on the ocean side of the ferry terminal, not on the street side," I said, I thought reasonably enough.

"He said he went to his car to get a jacket and that's when he saw it. According to him, he assumed Henry had left it running and gone in to use the facilities, and he couldn't resist playing a prank by driving your van to a different spot."

I rolled my eyes. I could just hear him trying to make himself sound like some good-kid-from-a-good-family-who-had-made-a-bad-choice-your-honor. "I'm not buying it. You know the size of that parking lot. I don't think it would be possible for anyone to see if a car has a driver from that distance. Plus, he would have to see through the ticket booths."

Chief Turner paused long enough to look at me and I felt he understood. Then he went on. "I said that was his *first* story. In his revised account, he said he knew he was inebriated and intended to walk to the beach adjacent to the ferry terminal. He said he hoped the ocean air would help him sober up, and that's when he saw the van."

Since On the Rocks is itself on the ocean, which comes in handy for the ferry to dock, I just shook my head.

"Finally he admitted he was headed to the beach hoping to meet, uh, someone to spend time with."

"Who?" I asked.

"I don't think he was particular—just anyone." He took off his cap and rubbed his hand over the top of his head. " That's when he saw the driverless van and got in it and moved it to the entry lane. And that is what the camera footage showed. We charged him with the vehicular crime, and he immediately made bail."

Lady Anthea turned to me. "You and I are the vehicular crime?"

I nodded. I'd been called worse.

"He left On the Rocks and had been drinking at the Crooked Hammock when he saw you two."

"What about Henry's shirt and the knife?" I asked, running my hand over the side of my head to get the hair out from under the side bar of my sunglasses.

"We haven't found either."

"Can't you get a search warrant for his home?" Lady Anthea asked.

"I doubt I'd be successful. The waitress says she can get as many people as we need to testify that Raymond Walton was right there from three o'clock on."

"I still think he's the murderer," Lady Anthea said. "Are we to believe that a coldblooded killer would leave the motor running—and therefore the air conditioner—in a van full of dogs out in the August sun, saving their lives, but that a veterinarian who was pulling a harmless prank would turn the engine off, endangering the animals' lives? Nonsense!" That word, spoken in British accent, has a lot of giddy-up in it.

"But, but—" Turner tried to get a word in.

"Because the van's ignition was off when Sue and I arrived," she continued.

"Yes, but—" When would the man learn? Lady Anthea would be done when she decided she was done.

"The dogs were barking when you telephoned Buckingham's, and I'll just bet they were barking when he got in the van." She shook a finger at him. "Don't let him say he didn't know the dogs were in there. He heard them and he knew. Dr. Walton is the killer," she concluded.

"I'm trying to tell you I agree," he said. "He was drunk last night and look what he did. You two could have been seriously hurt. And he was drinking for hours on Monday night. So, no, I'm not ruling him out." I couldn't see his eyes because of his sunglasses, but I saw the tension in his jaw. Problem was, he had been just this clear about Ashley Trent's guilt. So what was he, stubborn or thorough? My beginner's mind hadn't fixed on anyone.

"Did he toss Henry's phone out of the van?" I asked.

Chief Turner was pretty much worn out from Lady Anthea's presentation, and a shrug of his, admittedly broad, shoulders was all he could manage in the way of an answer.

"The phone indicates Henry was killed by someone he knew in some capacity, right?"

"Yeah," Chief Turner said.

"I'll go over Henry's emails to see if I can find a connection between him and Dr. Walton," I offered. "Did you ask him for the car keys? If he moved the car, he would have the car keys, right?"

"Hmm," Turner said. He *literally* scratched his head as he turned to walk away.

"So you forgot to ask him," Lady Anthea said.

Ouch, I thought.

"When you get that search warrant, maybe you'll find them," I said, that time out loud. I had spoken gently on account of his jangled nerves.

He nodded in reluctant acknowledgment and started moving again with long, purposeful strides.

"I have another question," I said.

Chief Turner backtracked the couple of paces he'd managed. Then he stood over me and waited.

"Why?" I asked.

"I told you. Because the waitress, or bartender, to be specific, alibied him."

"I meant, why did he run us off the road? Did he say?"

Abby sitting by my foot, looked at him, and waited patiently for an answer.

"He does seem to have a truckload of animosity toward you." He made it sound like a question.

"I always thought it was professional jealousy. It never occurred to me that it was personal. Well, at least not until now," I said.

"Will he be jailed since he has a previous?" Lady Anthea asked.

"Huh?" the chief asked.

Am I the only one who watches British crime shows? "We would say he has a *prior*. Like a prior conviction."

He shook his head. "That's up to the D.A. or maybe a jury, but I hope so."

Lady Anthea looked at me and gave me a sly smile. "Then here's another to help build your British slang vocabulary, *at her majesty's pleasure.*"

I took her arm and we walked by our uniformed friend. "He'll be doing the jailhouse rock," I said.

Chapter 14

Lady Anthea and I walked into a lobby filled with more pet parents than we'd seen at Buckingham's since Monday. Several of the swimmers had come back for a bath. Mason and Joey were scrambling to keep up with these walk-ins. I had rinsed Abby off at the beach water faucet, so I led her into my office, where she promptly fell asleep. Then I joined Shelby behind the counter to wait on the pet parents, settling their bills. Lady Anthea walked over to the tea table and poured a cup, but it wasn't for herself. She turned and held it out to Betsy Rivard, Paris and Riley's mom. "Would you care for a cup of tea? It's actually quite good."

Betsy was frozen speechless.

"I'm Lady Anthea Fitzwalter. We met Monday night." She held out the tea to her.

"I'm Paris. Oh, no, that's my dog. I'm Betsy Rivard." She laughed and took the tea.

Shelby had seen the exchange too and leaned over to whisper something to me. "Mrs. Rivard was one of the first people spreading the rumor about the dogs being stolen to be sold. Do you think we have her back on our side?"

"It sure looks like it," I answered.

"Business isn't as brisk as it was the days before the murder, but most of our regulars are back," Shelby said. "Charles Andrews is still holding out."

We both looked up when the door opened. "Hi, there, Dana," Shelby called out.

I went around to the customer side of the reception desk and hugged her. "Is your mother okay with you being here?"

"Uhhh," was her non-answer. Then she whispered, "My mom says I can't work here as long as there's a murderer on the loose."

"And she's right! There is a murderer on the loose!" Charles Andrews was a holdout no longer. Where had he come from? I hadn't even heard him come in. Speaking of hearing, he just had to pick that moment to regain his. Dana had whispered an inch from my ear. He stamped his cane on the tile floor. "You listen to your mother, young lady!" Technically, he was right since Henry's murderer hadn't been caught. Yet.

"Is that new police chief any good?" Betsy Rivard asked the room, in general.

"He's too young to know anything," Mr. Andrews said.

"He's in his forties," I replied. Actually, I was just guessing but that seemed about right. "He's learned a lot..."

"Like what?" I didn't know who had asked the question and it didn't much matter. I was looking at a sea of faces wanting the answer.

The outer front door was opened by a couple I didn't know. She was a middle-aged woman with dark brown hair, standing with a man with a serious-looking camera at the ready. I went to greet them at the inner doors. Thanks to the two doors, we've never lost a dog.

"Are you Sue Patrick?"

"Yes, I'm Sue."

"I'm Jane Burke from the *Southern Delaware Daily*. This is my husband, Michael. Would this be a good time for me to interview Lady Anthea?"

Well, yes and no. The arrival of the reporters would give the group something to talk about other than a murderer on the loose in Lewes, but what if it came up again?

"Could you point her out to us?" Jane continued, scanning the room.

Lady Anthea had already started walking toward me and the two mixed blessings people.

I introduced them and led them down the hall. My objective was to get them out of the lobby, specifically away from Charles Andrews. We turned left and went outside to the smaller of our two outdoor play areas, which was currently empty. A gentle breeze had kept the temperature and humidity low. "I thought this might be a good place to talk," I said to Jane. If they chose to sit to talk, there were wooden benches, one against each of the three high fences. Their height being another reason no runner has gotten away from us.

Michael scanned the blue climbing bridge with white foamy waves painted on its top edge, and the yellow wooden chair with *Lifeguard* stenciled on the back.

"Do you want to stand over there?" he asked Lady Anthea, pointing to the bridge. He was already looking through his lens.

She took one look at the play area furnishings and an eyebrow shot up. I jumped in, "I brought you out here for a quiet spot for the interview, but for the photograph maybe ..."

"I thought I could stand in front of my portrait *inside.*" Lady Anthea emphasized the last word.

He looked at Jane for salvation. "Sure!" she said. "Formal is good. Anything you say. We'd like to get back to the newspaper in time to get this in the online edition this afternoon."

Lady Anthea and I looked at each other. The sooner a complimentary article was published, the better. Now that all that was settled, Jane turned on an app on her phone to record the interview and smiled at her subject.

We had three objectives. First, to kill the rumor of the dogs being stolen once and for all. Second, to try to find out who started the rumor since it had started almost as soon as the body was found. And third, to get people to come to the gala. I moved to the side wall to listen and stay out of the way.

Anthea gave the history of our partnership in a nutshell and then talked about how well-cared for the dogs were at Buckingham's and how much fun they have. Jane asked her about the report of the dogs being the target of a theft and smuggling attempt and Lady Anthea pooh-poohed it.

"Could you turn off the recorder for a minute for a quick question?" she asked.

Jane obliged.

"How did you hear that rumor?"

"I can't reveal my source." She turned the recorder back on. When she resumed the interview, it was with a question about what was planned for entertainment at the gala.

I moved closer to Michael. "You know Dr. Walton was drunk when he phoned in that tip, don't you?"

His eyes widened and he gulped. Bingo.

Unfortunately, I had little time to celebrate my success in tricking the information out of him. "Are you thinking about suing us?" he asked.

"No! Where did that come from?"

"Thanks," he answered, ignoring my question.

It was time to see just how appreciative he was. "Did he say that Henry was dead in the back of the van?"

"No. He didn't *say* anything. Everything was phrased as a question," Michael responded. "When he called the first time, he asked why dogs had been left alone in the Buckingham van." Those words "first time" were the most important part of the sentence, as far as I was concerned. He had called the newspaper more than once. "He repeated that a couple of times. Then he called back to ask why they were being taken out of state. It would have been of interest since everyone in town knows you. Add to that Lady Anthea being here, and we pretty much knew we had to run it. Jane and I went to the ferry terminal when we got the first call to check it out, and that's when we saw the police activity. We got the second call while we were there."

Jane had gotten away from discussing the gala and was bombarding Lady Anthea with questions. My partner was arching her back to get away from the inquisition. "Are you in line for the throne?"

"No, I'm not!"

"Are you sure? Not even like, two-thousandth?"

"Oh, I'm quite sure."

"Have you ever been to Sandringham?"

"Yes. Uh, I mean." Lady Anthea obviously hadn't expected to talk about her royal connections.

"When?"

"For Christmas when I was a little girl," she answered in a low voice. "My grandmother was lady-in-waiting to the queen."

Jane's mouth dropped. "Did you wear plaid?" she squeaked.

"We wore tartan," Lady Anthea corrected her. "It was great fun. Just like the Pet Parent Appreciation Gala will be."

Jane looked over at me. "Some year, do you think we could wear *tartan*?" she cooed.

"I'm sure that could be arranged," Lady Anthea answered. Jane turned back to her, gratitude in her eyes. "If this year's gala is the success we anticipate, a *Sand*-ringham theme can certainly be planned for the future."

"Give us *all* the details you want us to put in the article," Jane said.

Lady Anthea and I did just that, and then she led them to the side gate to get back to their car in the parking lot. Naturally, we wanted to spare the reporter the unpleasant talk about having a murderer at large that might still be going on in the lobby.

"I'll look forward to reading the article," Lady Anthea said with a smile.

I held the whitewashed wooden gate open for them.

Michael stopped in his tracks, halfway through the opening. "What about the photograph of Lady Anthea?" He tapped the side of his camera, just in case any of us had forgotten that that's how you took photographs.

Ugh. So close yet so far away. I looked out at the parking lot. It wasn't as full as it had been earlier, now it was about a quarter full. Maybe Charles Andrews was gone.

I sheepishly reversed course and we went back inside. I could hear talking and laughing, but from the hallway I couldn't see anyone. When our little group reached the lobby, I spied Mason, Joey, and Dana standing in a half circle in the store section of the room. They had corralled Charles Andrews, Betsy Rivard, Kate Carter, and I couldn't see who else. Tucked away as they were, there would be no chatting about the murder with the reporter. Mason had them in stitches with a story about leaving a dog in one of the grooming suites to take a phone call and coming back to find that the dog had locked him out and locked himself in. My lead groomer comically detailed all the ways he tried to get the door unlocked before I found out. I hadn't heard this before, and I didn't want to hear it now, thank you very much. Still, it kept them occupied while Michael took a few formal, tasteful photographs of Lady Anthea standing in front of the portrait of her in the foyer at Frithsden, before the days of murder and vehicular crimes.

Chapter 15

As soon as everyone at Buckingham's had their lunch break, I asked Shelby for the use of her car, again, so we could pay Mary Jane Kerwin a visit. I had told Shelby about learning who Henry was seeing in last night's *the doctor is gin* session. She was rummaging through her handbag for her car keys when the owner of the garage called. The new airbags had been installed on the Jeep and I could pick the car up at my convenience.

"Lady Anthea, do you want to go with her and drive my car back?" Shelby asked.

"No!" I yelled. Could it be just two days since I had witnessed her driving skills, or lack of? It seemed like a lifetime ago.

"Driving here in the States is something I'll need to work on," Lady Anthea said. Shelby and I looked at each other. Lady Anthea hadn't been addressing anyone in particular. Still, it was an odd statement since her visit was already half over.

"Sue, I'll drive you," Shelby said. "Lady Anthea, we'll be gone just a few minutes. Could you answer the phone and greet anyone who comes in?"

"Sure," was the answer. She seemed genuinely happy to have the task.

"Mason and Joey are in back if anyone comes in for grooming. And call a nanny out if anything else comes up," I said.

"Nanny?"

"That's the employee in charge of the puppy playroom," I said on my way out.

As soon as we got in the car, Shelby started one of our quasi-telepathic conversations. "So?" she asked.

"That's what I was wondering too!" I answered.

"Would you be able to keep me if she stayed on in Lewes?" she asked, her brow creasing in worry.

"Of course," I said.

"Could you afford it?"

"We would figure out a way," I said. "Do you think she wants to stay? Why would she?"

"From what she said in there, and from what you've told me, it sounds like she might."

"If you had a house with a name, would you want to move here?" I asked.

"No! I mean, I love Lewes, but still. And it's not just Frithsden she'd be leaving. She's from a completely different world. I bet one piece of her jewelry could pay off the mortgages on both our houses. Sue, she knows the queen! She goes to openings and judges things. We work hard and she lives a life with servants to do everything for her." Shelby was on a roll.

"Actually, she doesn't have it as easy as we thought."

"Huh?"

"It seems her brother isn't exactly Merrill Lynch. He's made a mess of the family's finances," I explained.

"Whoa, just like the father in Downton Abbey," Shelby said.

"Pretty close," I agreed.

***

Our visit to Mary Jane Kerwin was unannounced because we didn't want to give her time to make up an alibi or slip out the backdoor or anything. Lady Anthea and I had discussed it on the short drive through town after I was reunited with my Jeep. We wanted to see the look on her face when we told her that there was another woman in Henry's future. We tried to think of a way to start the conversation and hadn't gotten far.

"We know you were sleeping with the victim and we were just wondering if you killed him, doesn't hit the right note, does it?" I pointed out.

"Well, how do they start these discussions in those mysteries you love?" she asked. "What were you reading last night?"

"That was *To Think a Thought of Murder*. Want it when I finish?"

"Thank you but, no."

To each his own. "I understand. I think everyone should read what they want to read. Just like you should eat what you want to eat. But I digress. In the books I read, more times than not, the killer or a suspect catches the amateur sleuth poking his or her nose where it doesn't belong and threatens something bad if they don't stop. Then the detective says why did you kill so-and-so, and the other guy either says I didn't, or he tells why he killed the person. I don't think any of that is going to help us today, though."

We drove on awhile, with her looking out the window.

"What do you like to read?" I asked.

"I'm re-reading volume one of Howard Carter's *The Tomb of Tutankhamun*, now that it's available as an e-book."

"If you've read it before, you know how it turns out. He found King Tut."

"Let's just say I love reading how life can surprise you." Then she did this half snort, half laugh thing, which I think means she thought that was funny. Anyway, we needed to get back to talking about our looming interview with Mary Jane Kerwin. "I almost forgot. The newspaper photographer confirmed our suspicion. It was Dr. Walton who phoned them about the van being left unattended on the road near the ferry terminal."

"So he's the murderer!" she said.

"Actually, he told them there were dogs left alone in our van, and he started the rumor about the attempt to take them out of state, but he didn't mention the murder. It was that call that got the reporter and the photographer to the ferry terminal, and they took it from there once they saw the police," I said.

"So he's guilty of making Buckingham's look as bad as possible," Lady Anthea said. I agreed and then she went on. "His loathing of you might be a motive."

"Ouch. Isn't loathing a little strong?"

"Very well, have it your way, his dislike of you. Have you considered that?" she asked.

"Are you sure you're not reading my mysteries?"

"Quite sure. Are you going to tell Chief Turner?"

After considering this for a few minutes I said, "Sure, why not?" When I caught a red light, I flipped through my recent calls on my cell phone until I came to his number. He picked up on the second ring.

"Hello, Sue." If I live to be one hundred, I'll never get used to being on the receiving end of caller ID. For some reason that deep voice almost made me giggle. No idea why.

I told him about Dr. Walton calling the *Southern Delaware Daily* to the Monday night goings on.

"I'll note that, but I already knew he wasn't a fan of yours or of the Pet Place—"

"Pet Palace," I corrected.

"Yeah, whatever. My first clue was how he tried to kill you last night. So now you believe what I said about not being their source?"

"Yeah, whatever," I mimicked.

"Have you uncovered anything else I can use?"

"Yeah, I have an overflowing treasure trove of clues I'm holding back from you. Thought I'd dispense them one phone call at a time."

"Very funny," he said with a chuckle. "I happen to know you want the murderer behind bars and everybody's peace of mind restored before Friday night."

"That's not the only reason. Justice for Henry might be nice," I said.

"At least we have something in common. Where are you now?"

"At Buckingham's," I lied.

"Sue, you're traveling east on Savannah Road."

I rubbed my neck. My collar was too tight. I felt like my clothes had turned on me. "Why did you ask me if you already knew?" I yelled then I hung up. My seatbelt was bothering me too, and I yanked at it. It wasn't like I didn't know the police had technology at their fingertips. A literary person like myself was going to know that. But if I wanted Chief Turner, or anyone else, to know where I was or where I was going, I would tell them.

Lady Anthea didn't give me much time to calm down. "Are you really that indignant or did you hang up because you were afraid he was about to ask if we had the name of the woman Henry was seeing?"

"Not much gets past you," I said with a laugh.

"There's more to it than that, though. Isn't there? That really bothered you."

"I feel like he's trying to trap me. I mean, track me." I lowered my sunglasses from the top of my head to a more practical location, that being in front of my eyes.

We had crossed the bridge over the canal, and I turned left off of Savannah Road onto Massachusetts Avenue. "We'll take the first right," I said to Lady Anthea.

We arrived at Mary Jane's A-frame house by passing it twice, going to the end of the street and coming back, twice. "I don't think she's at home," Lady Anthea said. The fact that there was no car in the driveway and there was no garage, was what had prompted this Sherlock Holmes deduction. I parked on the street across from the house since that's the way I was facing coming from my last foray down to its end, and we walked up the short driveway. A curving flagstone path led to the front door.

"Let's go and knock on the door anyway, just to be sure," I suggested.

A porch stretched across the front of the house. A striped hammock and two Adirondack chairs, painted royal blue, pretty much filled it. I knocked once and stopped, my knuckles hovering. I had spied something of interest. Still, I needed to be sure she wasn't at home before I did what I was thinking I couldn't possibly do. I knocked again and waited, listening. By that time, Lady Anthea knew something was up. "I don't hear anything, do you?" I whispered.

She shook her head, no, and looked around.

I took this as approval from the universe, and from her, to reach into Mary Jane's mailbox and take the letters out. One envelope was from WSFS, Wilmington Savings Fund Society. "This is a local bank," I explained. "A lot of local businesses use them. We call it WISFIS." I tried to see through the envelope, then around the plastic window. No luck.

"I see Ms. Kerwin has one of those outdoor showers," Lady Anthea said. She'd been scanning the perimeter when she noticed it.

I absentmindedly agreed as I tried to look under the envelope flap.

"Do you think we could steam the envelope open with hot water from it?" Lady Anthea asked.

That got my attention—and admiration. "Depends on what kind of system she has," I said as I left the porch and walked around to the outdoor shower. The wooden slats were painted to match the house color. The opening was in the rear; and we walked around to it and looked inside.

"I don't see a way to steam the envelope without us and the statement getting soaked, but, nice try."

"Do these bank statements ever get lost in the post?" she asked.

"Rarely, but I guess it could happen." Before I could finish my sentence, she grabbed the envelope out of my hand, stepped through the opening to the shower stall, and ripped it open.

"It just happened to Ms. Kerwin."

I joined her in the cubicle and stared at the defiled envelope. "You just opened someone's mail." I stared in disbelief at what I'd just seen.

"You were trying to see inside. Is there a difference?"

"Uh, yeah," I said without much conviction. You could say the difference was that with my method, Mary Jane Kerwin would never know. In the stratosphere where Lady Anthea operated, it never occurred to her that she wasn't allowed to rip open someone else's mail if she wanted to. She was born into that world and had known no other.

As she read the first page, her eyes widened. "Is it typical to have a balance this high in this type of account?" she asked.

I looked over her shoulder. "No, most people don't have a checking account balance with that many figures." I scanned down the page and whistled. A fifty-thousand-dollar deposit had been made three weeks ago.

"Didn't the couple last night say she worked part-time at the Best of the Past? Would that be as lucrative as this would indicate?"

"I don't see how," I answered. "Wonder what else she does? She hasn't lived here very long, so I don't know her well. I saw her once or twice when she brought her puppy to Buckingham's." My eyes were glued to the paper in Lady Anthea's hand. "I don't know where she lived before moving to Lewes."

We heard a car coming down the street and getting closer, with its radio blasting Beach Boys music. I pivoted and looked through half-inch slits between the wooden boards. "What kind of person plays Beach Boys music at that volume?" I whispered.

Lady Anthea shot me a look.

"Honestly, I want to know. The two just don't go together."

This time she shushed me.

I saw a young woman in a red Corvette convertible, top down, slowing. That's who. Too bad I would probably never get to ask her to explain. "That's her," I whispered. "It's Mary Jane Kerwin."

We heard tires on the gravel drive. Unwelcome noises are louder when you're holding your breath, the way we were. Lady Anthea looked down at our feet and my eyes followed hers. There was about a foot of daylight between the ground and the wall of the outdoor shower. Still, the shower was far enough back on the side of the house, that unless she came around and looked in, she wouldn't see us. I tapped Lady Anthea on the arm and then pointed at my car on the opposite side of the road, instead of in front of Mary Jane's house. She gave me a thumbs-up and we grinned at each other. It looked like someone was visiting the house across the street. We heard the front door open and that meant all we had to do was wait a few more seconds then we would be home free. Lady Anthea stuffed the purloined mail into her handbag. We turned back to the opening to wait until it was safe to tread back to the Jeep.

Then we heard the back door open, and judging by the slam, there was a screen door too. Next something heavy, with toenails, scampered out. Our presence in her outdoor shower may have escaped Mary Jane Kerwin's notice, but her Saint Bernard puppy knew we were there. I motioned for Lady Anthea to move to the side so we wouldn't be standing in front of the opening, just in case Mary Jane walked around the house with her dog. We watched through the slats as he galloped toward us, panting so heavy that each exhale sounded like, "Who, who." Really. It wasn't my guilty conscience imagining it.

I hadn't seen this sixty- or seventy-pound guy since he'd attended Puppy 101 at Buckingham's, and for the life of me I couldn't remember his name. I certainly knew nothing about his temperament. Was he aggressive or a sweetie pie? I took a deep breath. "I'll distract him while you run to the Jeep."

She looked at me, neither nodding acquiescence nor shaking her head refusing.

I steeled myself to step into the opening but before I could, the back door scraped open, again followed by the screen door slamming shut.

"Whiskey?" the woman called out.

Unless she was placing an order for a drink, I had the dog's name. He stopped his charge toward us and turned around. He seemed to weigh his options and, sorry, decided we were the more interesting choice.

She called his name again, but this time the dog didn't turn around, he just kept walking to us.

I had placed myself in front of Lady Anthea and turned my head to her. "I'm going out now. You need to go to the Jeep!"

She was looking out from the wall. "There's the owner."

I joined her lookout. My first thought was "so that's who Henry cheated on his fiancée with." It had been almost a year since Mary Jane Kerwin had brought her puppy to Buckingham's, but she looked about the same, if anything, a little harder around the edges.

"Whiskey! You come here right now! I have to go to work." Ms. Kerwin had her hand on her hip.

The dog looked at the shower stall and then back at her. Then he sat, which is the default action a lot of young dogs use when they don't know what to do. It's a command they have down pat. It was also a clue that very little training had taken place after the puppy classes he'd had with us.

She stamped her foot. "Fine! Just stay there for all I care," she yelled, turning on her heel and walking back the way she'd come. I noticed the soles of her shoes were red. Since I didn't live under a rock, I knew that was the trademark of some designer. Not that I could have told you which one. "You stupid idiot dog," she yelled as a parting shot.

I squeezed my eyes shut in reaction to the unfairness of what she'd said. I wanted to yell out that she was the one who hadn't found time to train her dog, and that wasn't the dog's fault.

Whiskey was in a ready-sit position, and he was looking back and forth between Mary Jane's back and the outdoor shower. The screen door slammed and he whimpered. I stepped out and went to him.

"It's okay," I whispered, as I slowly approached him. He didn't stand, but he wagged his tail, swishing it on the grass. I reached over to let him smell my hand and then I petted him. "Good boy."

Then I started walking toward the back of the house, stopping after a few feet to look back at him. "Come," I said, still in a whisper. He jumped up and followed me. I took his collar and turned him to the porch, petted him one more time, and then nudged him in that direction. He looked at me again and then went to the door.

"Okay, I thought if I left you sitting there you'd get up and come in," snarled his owner. "Maybe you'll know better next time."

Lady Anthea was peering out the shower door, and I sprinted back to join her. She tilted her head and whispered, "Sue, I think you work magic on dogs."

"Thanks." I looked out into the yard, playing it off like I needed to check that Whiskey hadn't changed his mind and come back. Obviously, this wasn't the case since he was already in the house. The truth was that I was touched by her compliment. I turned back to her. "I was just thinking that since we came here to talk to her, why don't we go to the front door and knock now?"

"Brilliant," she said. "She wouldn't know which direction we walked from."

"Let me catch my breath and we can casually stroll up to the door." I leaned back. "Ho-o-o!" I had rested against the faucet and turned the water on. Very cold water poured down on me. The temperature paralyzed my mouth in the open position.

Lady Anthea, expensive clothes be damned, lunged forward to put her hand over my mouth to keep the sound I was exhaling from becoming audible. With the other, she yanked me away from the knob. Though I was still in shock from surprise and from the cold water, and sputtering vowels, I managed to reach back and turned it off. "I'm so sorry," I mouthed. I would throw my khaki shorts and Buckingham polo shirt in the washing machine, but she was wearing a silk blouse. Even her pearl necklace had gotten wet.

"So much for casually strolling to the front..." Lady Anthea stopped speaking. The front door had opened and closed.

Neither of us breathed as we waited to hear Mary Jane Kerwin come down the porch steps and around the corner. It was just a matter of time before we were busted, so I started coming up with a story to explain what we were doing in her outdoor shower. After less than a minute we heard her car start. Lady Anthea and I smiled at each other. Another embarrassment averted.

When the noise of the car engine died out, we left our hiding spot, and, hanging our heads, went back to the Jeep.

"That was refreshing," Lady Anthea said.

I gave a little half laugh, but I was wondering how to interpret her remark. I'm no stranger to sarcasm. Actually, we're quite close. I may have been overthinking what she'd said, but now that I knew the real state of Lady Anthea's finances, that her involvement with the Pet Palace wasn't just a hobby, I was even more worried that if this craziness continued she might want to cut her losses and sell out. After all our long hours, Shelby, Mason, Joey, Dana, and I had forged a go-down-with-the-ship loyalty to Buckingham's, but Lady Anthea had been someone who sent us school teacher emails.

Chapter 16

An hour later, Lady Anthea and I walked into the Best of the Past, hair and makeup repaired, clothes changed, pearls around at least one of our necks. The store was situated across from St. Peter's Episcopal Church, but since it was Wednesday we found a parking spot nearby, without too much driving around and circling. We walked the half block down Mulberry Street, which is perpendicular to Second. A bell rang overhead when the door opened, and Peter Collins was standing in front of us before the jingling died away. The guard dog greeting made me think he'd watched through the glass front as we'd walked down the hill. A group of four tourists, two women and two men, browsed in the main section of the store.

"Remember, he said this was both an antiques store and an art gallery. Guess this is the store part." The room was filled with display cases of thimbles, jewelry, and vintage toys. Book cases with dusty volumes lined the side walls.

I saw two older women take a left down the hallway that gave the store its L-shape floor plan, but I didn't see Mary Jane Kerwin. Behind me Lady Anthea was making nice with the proprietor, Peter, but there's only so much obsequiousness one person can take and when she had her limit, she took my arm and led me away. "Sue and I would love to look around."

Not one to take a hint, Peter followed us. We covered the main part of the business and then sauntered to the back area. We weren't only trying to shake him; we were still looking for Mary Jane.

"We refer to this section as our art gallery," he said, walking around to get in the lead, like a tour guide.

The two customers passed Lady Anthea and me on their way out. The woman closest to me leaned over. "She's not very friendly," she whispered. I looked down the narrow room to see who *she* was. Mary Jane Kerwin was staring at us. I told my guilty conscience to shut up. It wasn't like she knew we stole her bank statement out of her mailbox or had trespassed in her shower.

It seemed Lady Anthea had the same affliction because she had a death grip on her shoulder bag, lest anything, like correspondence from a bank, should jump out. Mary Jane looked to the right, then to my left, like she was looking for the best escape route. Obviously, she didn't want to talk to us. Too bad, because Lady Anthea and I still needed to talk to her about her clandestine relationship with Henry. I stretched out my hand and approached her. "Hi! Mary Jane Kerwin, right? You're Whiskey's mom?"

Her red-orange lip curled at the *mom* part. "Yes, Whiskey is my dog."

"I don't know if you remember me. I'm Sue Patrick from Buckingham Pet Palace," I said. Her four-inch heels raised her up to my height, but for some reason, in her painted-on red dress, she seemed to tower over me. I briefly wondered if she was physically able to overpower Henry, drugged or not.

The space was reserved for ornately framed paintings, photography, and a drawing or two. Several had cards stuck into a bottom corner announcing the piece was "on hold," or "sold." There was no overhead lighting nor windows, instead small spotlights were aimed at the artwork that lined both walls. An interior decorator would say the difference in lighting between this room and the larger one was to make the side room a separate space from the main sales floor, without going to the trouble of building a physical wall.

The low level of lighting was putting me on edge. The only way I could describe it was that it gave me the feeling there was someone or something around me, but outside my field of vision. It wasn't just having Peter Collins on our heels, either. Maybe if I got to work questioning Mary Jane, I would calm down. Now if only Mr. Collins would go on about his business.

"So, you work here?" I asked.

She gave me a "duh" look of exasperation, which I guess I deserved. Why else would she be there talking to customers? But was the attitude really necessary? I could be in the market for antiques or a nice painting for all she knew. Finally, she answered with a nod.

"She's indispensable to me," Collins said.

Lady Anthea and I turned and he continued. "Ms. Kerwin is both my accountant and my art buyer." He beamed at her, and she looked more than a little uncomfortable. "Sue, since you're here, may I ask you something?"

"Sure."

He led us farther into the room and Mary Jane had to back up. She had been standing in front of a large oil painting of a man wearing knee-high boots, sitting on a rock with two dogs jumping around and having a grand old time behind him. By oil painting, I mean oil painting or watercolor, or something. A "sold" sign tucked into the frame. Collins was finally silent, wearing a smile I couldn't interpret, and waiting for our reaction to the artwork.

As I took in the painting, I became aware of Lady Anthea standing beside me, but leaning closer and closer still to the piece of art. Though her mouth was open, she didn't seem to be breathing.

"Are you okay?" I asked.

She turned and looked at Peter Collins. "Is this what I think it is?" Her voice was low, and she dispensed the words one by one, her eyes were wide as Abby's water bowls. I looked at the work of art again, but slowly. I took in the paint colors, and the colors within colors, and I wanted to *be* there, just walk into it.

Peter Collins flung his hand in the direction of her new treasure. "This? It's suitable for a bachelor pad. Or are they called man caves these days?" I didn't do a Daniel Webster on him about the correct definition of *man cave* because I think people who do that are obnoxious. And because I think he knew that. He'd spoken so quickly, almost chattering.

He was pointing back and forth to the painting and to its partner on the right, a landscape that also included a few dogs and a couple of fine looking horses. By landscape, I mean land was portrayed somewhere on the canvas. The two were the same size, maybe three feet wide and four feet tall. "I inherited these two, plus one other, but as I've been informed, sentimental value is all they have." He paused and looked over my shoulder at Mary Jane. "I'm afraid my knowledge of art isn't what it should be. They've been in my family for years, and I thought they were a good start to this addition of an art gallery to my antiques store. They're fun, aren't they?"

Fun? Lady Anthea looked like she was in the presence of greatness. She was back to staring at the painting. I was curious about her reaction and couldn't wait to hear what was behind it. I turned my attention to the second painting and found it just as compelling as its mate.

Peter Collins reached out and tapped the sold card on the first painting and when he spoke again, what he said delivered a shock to all three of us. "Henry was the buyer. Should I deliver it to Buckingham's?"

"Henry?" The word flew out of my mouth, an involuntary reaction like a cough.

"Henry!" Lady Anthea's voice was so loud it sounded like she was calling him for dinner.

All Mary Jane could say was, "Uhhh."

Peter looked at Lady Anthea and then at me. "Yes, Henry had already purchased the first in the group from me, and this one also."

The idea of my slacker employee as an art collector, if buying two paintings qualifies one as a collector, would take some getting used to. Frankly, the artwork seemed above his taste level—it was certainly above mine—but Lady Anthea was truly shocked.

Mary Jane was frowning at the painting that sported the sold sign, and now she walked up to it and reached around the top right corner. "Has this been moved recently?" The stern tone said somebody had some explaining to do. She made some kind of adjustment to the way the painting was mounted, then pulled back to evaluate the result. I guess it was A-OK, because next she turned her attention to Peter Collins. She lowered her head and glowered at him. The effect was not unlike a bull communicating with a matador. "It hasn't been paid for," she said, answering her boss's question.

At this, Collins jerked his head away from us to face her. "My mistake. I was not aware of that." Declarations of war have been made with less venom than what I heard in those two sentences. He had bared his teeth into what we were supposed to think was a smile.

The undercurrents in the room had undercurrents. I had no idea what was behind any of it, and I hoped my business partner did.

"I might be interested in taking it off your hands," Mary Jane said.

Her boss didn't seem to have a response to this relatively straight-forward remark.

If Peter Collins played background music in his store, Elvis's "A Little Less Conversation" would fit my mood. I'd had enough of their verbal duals so I put my hand on the arm of the one person in the vicinity I could trust not to take a bite out of it. "Lady Anthea, have you told Mr. Collins about your interview with the newspaper?" I turned and smiled at him, ready to bet good money I was better at the phony grin thing than he ever thought about being. "She told them about her grandmother being lady-in-waiting to the queen. Fascinating."

My partner moved around me and led him back to the main sales floor, then suddenly she stopped and came back. At some point she'd let her handbag slip to the floor, accidently on-purpose, I'd guess. "I almost forgot this," she said with a little laugh. I knelt to get it for her and she leaned over me. "Use your phone to take a photograph of both of these," she whispered.

I watched Lady Athena and Peter Collins walk out and then turned back to look at the paintings again, the one that either had or had not been purchased by Henry Cannon and the similar one hanging next to it, letting their beauty refresh my eyes.

Ms. Kerwin moved to stand next to me. We were closer than I cared for, what with her being one of our murder suspects. There seemed to be more adjustments needed because now her hand was under the lower corner of the frame of the first painting and she was fiddling around back there. There was probably some art world term for what she was doing, but since Lady Anthea was in the other room of the store, that technical point would have to be a mystery to me a little longer.

"Someone has moved this painting," she muttered. As soon as she finished whatever she was doing, she gave the painting one last appreciative look and moved back. The look on her face told me she was getting antsy and would soon make a break for open spaces.

"You haven't lived in Lewes long, have you?" I asked to stop her.

"I lived here a few years back when I attended the School of Nursing at Beebe. I'm enjoying being back in Lewes," she said. The last sentence was spoken without feeling, and I was betting added out of relief that I hadn't asked about Henry. Yet.

"You're a nurse?"

"Yes, an R.N. but I haven't practiced in a year or so. Not that that has ever stopped anyone and everyone from hitting me up for free medical advice."

"I understand you and Henry Cannon were friends."

Her head jerked at the abrupt subject change. "I met him. He certainly didn't deserve what happened to him." Again, there was no emotion in her voice.

"More than friends," I continued.

She turned to me with a shocked look on her face. "I don't know where you got your information—"

I interrupted her before she could insult my intelligence with the denial. "I know about your relationship."

Again, the look of shock, this time with a bit of hurt. Since I'm new at this detective stuff, I couldn't tell if she expected me to fall for that, but she was a good actress, giving credit where credit's due. But then, why hadn't she used her stage skills to pretend to have a little emotion over Henry's death?

I almost added in a my-sympathy-during-this-difficult-time-for-you phrase, but I'd had enough playacting for one day. Besides, if she killed Henry, her life was going to get a lot more difficult.

She squinted, looking me up and down, to telegraph her opinion of my khaki shorts, Buckingham polo shirt, and leather sandals. I longed to tell her my ego had been safe from people like her for years.

"You don't know anything," she sneered.

She was right that there was a lot I didn't know. For example, I had no idea how Henry could have been attracted to two women as different as Ashley and her. Nor did I know what this woman could have seen in young, immature Henry. "I *know* the police chief's phone number. When I give him your name, you'll be a person of interest."

"What? I didn't kill him!" Both her face and her voice had run the gamut of emotions. She'd betrayed anxiety, just short of fear. Maybe laced with a bit of threat.

"I was here working Monday, almost all day. I usually just work afternoons but since Peter was away I came in early."

I looked down and shook my head. I was unwilling to take anything she said at face value. "When did you come back to Lewes?"

"About six months ago. Why do you ask?"

I thought back to what Ashley had said at the police station. Henry's extra funds had come in very soon after he moved to Lewes, which was three months ago. "You knew Henry before he moved here, didn't you?"

"No, we met when I brought my dog to Buckingham's."

"Henry wasn't working for me when Whiskey came for puppy training."

"I don't remember where we met." She swung her hand out, like she was swatting an annoying fly. "Just some place in town."

"Let me ask you again, did you know Henry before he moved here?"

Actually, I didn't have *all* the information I needed to jump to that. I didn't yet know if the deposit we'd seen on her bank statement coincided with his. The source of her healthy bank account could be commissions earned here at the Best of the Past or could have come from any number of ventures that had nothing to do with Henry. But how was Henry making money? He was smooth and good looking, but not nearly as smart as he thought he was. Mary Jane was shrewd. I could see her being the brains behind any operation the two of them might have been involved in. She must have needed him for something—that would explain what she was doing with a guy like Henry.

She hesitated a beat. I'd hit a nerve.

"Where did you meet him?"

Mary Jane gave her head two quick shakes. "Look, I'll admit we were *seeing* each other. People get together. Things happen." There it was. She'd landed on manipulation. She'd decided to play this like we were BFFs and this was girl talk.

I didn't even try to stop the eye roll. "Oh, come on. Our society runs on euphemisms, I get that. You were dating him to use him." It hadn't escaped my notice that my question about when and where they'd met had gone unanswered. I didn't repeat it because I didn't expect the truth. Chief Turner would just have to do a background check.

"I didn't know he was engaged. I ended it when I found out."

Well, that was either true or it wasn't, I thought.

I heard the fawning voice of Peter Collins getting closer and turned to get his ETA. He was still in the larger room. Instead, I saw two men coming to see the row of paintings. They began ooh-ing and ah-ing. After giving me one last scowl, Mary Jane rearranged her expression and approached them. Then her overly made-up eyes landed on something or someone past them and she raised an eyebrow. Her lips pursed then formed a very different kind of smile. "Hello there," she cooed.

I turned to see it was Chief Turner who was the recipient of her efforts. If she was guilty, I would have thought someone in a police uniform would be about the last person she'd want to see sauntering in. He glanced at her and then continued walking back to me. She looked at him with narrowed eyes, then glared at me before moving on to her customers.

I slipped my phone out of my pocket and snapped two photos of each of the pieces of artwork that Collins had described as "fine for a bachelor's apartment" but had mesmerized Lady Anthea. I thought about their differing assessments and decided to put my money, assuming I had any after the gala, on Lady Anthea. I had no idea why she wanted photographs of the paintings, but I was sure she had her reasons.

"Somehow I never thought you'd be an art lover." I was ready for the deep voice and this time it hadn't made me jump.

"I can't talk," I said. I didn't want Peter Collins nor Mary Jane Kerwin, who was still answering questions from the two customers, to see me taking the photographs.

He looked up and down the room. "Why not?"

"I'm on a case," I answered, just to make him mad.

"You don't have a case." He glanced around again for any prying ears, then said in a low voice, "I need to ask you about something we found when we searched the victim's residence."

I heard Mary Jane telling her customers about a drawing on the back wall that they simply must see. She pointed the way and the three walked past us, only when Mary Jane moved behind Chief Turner, she didn't have quite enough room and had to press against his back.

"Pardon me," he said, moving closer to me.

"I have information for you," I said when they were out of earshot.

"That's the girlfriend, I take it?" he asked.

I nodded.

"Anything else I should know?" he whispered in my ear.

I shrugged. By that I meant, *you'll have to wait until I can figure out how to tell you she came into a lot of money without admitting to stealing her mail.*

"Can you tell me the rest over dinner?" His words were clipped and he sounded unsure of his footing.

"You don't have a chance," I said and walked around him.

Chapter 17

On the drive back to Buckingham's, I told Lady Anthea what I'd learned. "I guess we wasted our time. She has an alibi. She was working when Henry was killed."

"That's interesting," Lady Anthea said.

"Not really. Most people work," I said.

"I meant, Peter Collins was out of town on Monday, so how do we know she was at the gallery?"

"I guess we could ask her for the names of any customers who saw her," I said.

"You mean, the police can ask her," Lady Anthea corrected me.

"That's fine with me. We have a business to look after. I took the photographs like you asked. I thought the paintings were amazing, but you heard how Peter Collins described them. Why are you interested? Because they included dogs?"

"Hardly. I suspect…"

Before she could say more, my phone pinged to let me know a new text had come in. Since traffic was building on Savannah Road, I handed it to my passenger. "Would you read this?"

"It's from Shelby," she said. "Oh, my!"

"That doesn't sound like Shelby."

"No, that was from me. Here's what Shelby wrote: *Come back. Now. Ashley is here. Mad. Yelling.*"

The posted speed limit along Savannah Road changes block by block, and police cruisers tucked away on side streets and beside buildings give the signs gravitas. You see enough drivers getting tickets and you realize these are more than mere suggestions for the motoring public. I wanted to floor the accelerator, but I knew better. Getting stopped would cost me more time than I would gain.

"I need you to talk to Shelby and find out what's happening. Tell her we're on our way."

"I'll call her. You get us back to Buckingham's!"

I looked over to see if she knew how to telephone someone back from a text, but she was already placing the call. She caught me looking.

"I know how." She held the phone to her ear. "Just because I live in a two-hundred-year-old house doesn't mean I don't have a smart phone. Shelby, it's Anthea." She told her we were nearby. Then she put Shelby on speaker phone.

"It was her! It was her!" Ashley Trent shouted in the background.

"We're in your office with the door closed," Shelby whispered.

Both Lady Anthea and I exhaled in relief that whatever this was, it wasn't playing out in the lobby in front of pet parents.

"What was her?" I asked.

"I can't get her to tell me," Shelby said.

I turned into the Villages of Five Points and made the left into our parking lot. Lady Anthea was running in almost before the Jeep had come to a complete stop and I wasn't far behind. Although it was almost five, the lobby was calm. Dana was handling the desk. She smiled sweetly at her customer, but when she caught my eye, I could tell her tranquility was for show. I was proud of her for being so professional, and at such a young age.

Lady Anthea and I opened the door to my office and closed it behind us as quickly as we could. We had just entered the epicenter of the chaos.

Ashley was pacing the five or six feet of open space in the compact room. Her eyes were flashing and her hands were balled into fists. Shelby was standing back behind the desk. She'd put Abby on the desk chair, out of harm's way. Ashley turned when I walked in and inhaled a gulp of air. She paused at the top of the breath and prepared to unleash her anger.

"Ashley?" I said, before she could speak. "What's going on?" I was going for soothing, but I didn't know how long I could keep that up. Temper tantrums were for children, not grownups.

"It was you!" she yelled.

"What was me?" Under the circumstances a reasonable query, I thought.

"You were having an affair with my fiancé!" she yelled. "I knew something was going on down here, but he kept telling me I was crazy, that I was just being silly."

For a second I thought she was saying I'd had an affair with her fiancé. Dammit, that's exactly what she'd said. I didn't know where to start telling her how ludicrous that was, but I was getting close. Then I was diverted by my own thoughts. Had Chief Turner told her about Henry's in-town girlfriend?

Lady Anthea stepped in front of me. "How did you find out, my dear?"

I wasn't sure whose head jerked to Lady Anthea fastest, mine or Shelby's. Had she lost her mind too?

"The police let me in Henry's apartment. They looked through everything. This afternoon they said I could start packing up. *Date with boss, date with boss* was all over a calendar he kept in one of his drawers," she yelled.

I closed my eyes, but for just a second because I was still in a room with a crazy person. So that's what Chief Turner was talking about when he said he wanted to ask me about something they found during their search of Henry's home. "But it wasn't me," I said and pinched the bridge of my nose. Just the thought of what my life had turned into this week made me wonder if I would ever be back on my surfboard again.

Ashley looked at Lady Anthea. "She had to pay him to— to— to do whatever they did! Did you know that?"

Lady Anthea's tightlipped stare expressed the shock she'd suffered at what she'd let loose. On the other end of the spectrum, I was afraid Shelby was going to burst out laughing. She knows better than anyone what an unencumbered life I live. The idea that I would pay for sex was crazy.

Lady Anthea moved closer to Ashley and stood in front of her to stop that irritating pacing. "Dear, how did you find out about that?" Granted, we learned something helpful the last time she asked that question, but I was feeling a bit picked on.

"I found his checkbook and his pay stubs." Here Ashley turned on me again. "You weren't paying him very much, you know. I mean, for his salary." The last word came out *saal-ah-reeee.*

Of course, I knew how much we paid him. "I never claimed to pay him a fortune; that came from you," I said.

"Do you know what he wrote by the deposit for his bonus?"

"No idea."

"*Payment from boss.* That's what he wrote."

Lady Anthea took Ashley by her shoulders. "Ms. Trent, I think we might very well have a case of mistaken identity here. I don't believe your fiancé was having an affair with Sue."

I mentally thanked her.

Ashley hung her head. I hoped when she raised it again, I would hear an apology. Instead, she said, "She was his boss! Who else could it be?"

I was beginning to think we'd indulged this young woman long enough. I wanted to check the night shift in. I didn't know how long Dana could work considering her mother's fear for her safety. I caught Shelby looking at her watch. She probably wanted to get home to Jeffrey and her own dogs.

"Think about it," Shelby said, leaning over the back of my desk chair. Ashley turned to face her. "What would Henry want with her when he had an attractive, young wife-to-be like you?" She jerked a thumb in my general direction.

Wait. That was my best friend sticking up for me?

"Yeah," Ashley said, after glancing over at me. "I guess you're right."

"Of course, she is," Lady Anthea cooed.

What was this *of course* business?

"Except I have further proof!" Ashley said, still in a huff. *Here we go again.*

"What might that be?" I asked, letting the annoyance come through.

"When Chief Turner called to tell me about Henry being dead, he thought I was his sister, not his fiancée. Why would Henry say that on his job application? He didn't want you to know about me!"

I threw up my hands. "Well, looks like you got me," I said.

Lady Anthea moved to stand in front of me, but not before giving me a reprimanding look.

"Of course." Lady Anthea paused to bestow upon Ashley a sympathetic smile. "There's the possibility that date with boss, simply meant he had an appointment with Sue." Her tone said, *stand back I'm working here.*

"No!" Ashley was back to pacing. "He got home late almost every night. He was writing in code in case I saw it."

"Good luck, Ms. Trent. It's too bad we can't help you find the identity of the person." Lady Anthea was slowly moving toward the door as she spoke. She was reaching for the knob when she turned her head and gave Ashley a *what a shame* look. I was beginning to get suspicious of my business partner's sincerity. Like the lifeline she'd thrown Ashley was short by a few feet and that had been intentional.

"But you could! I bet you could if you wanted to," Ashley called out. She pointed to Shelby and then reluctantly to me. "They know everyone in town. That's what Henry told me."

Lady Anthea shook her head. "I can't imagine how that would help you. Unless…" She let the word drop.

"Unless what?" Ashley picked it up, just as Lady Anthea had intended.

"Well, perhaps if we looked through Henry's belongings, something might occur to Sue."

There it was. Lady Anthea had played her like a violin. She was good.

"Sure!" Ashley sounded delighted. "I mean, the police took some stuff, but you can look at what's left."

"We'll come to his apartment and do just that, dear. Are you staying there now, or are you and Lion King still at the hotel?" Lady Anthea asked.

"We're at the hotel. I've packed up some of Henry's things already. I can bring the boxes over here tomorrow," Ashley offered.

"No," I said.

"No," Shelby said at the same time. We didn't need her pitching another fit in our lobby, thank you very much.

Lady Anthea smiled sweetly. "Ashley, you've been through so much. We'll come to you in the morning." Then she opened the door and ushered the young woman out.

Chapter 18

At eight o'clock that night, Lady Anthea, Shelby, and I were sitting in my screened-in porch. Shelby had depicted the summit to Jeffrey as a business meeting. A Grotto pizza box and a big tossed salad took up most of the wrought iron dining table. I had a death grip on my glass of Chianti as I listened to Lady Anthea talk about the paintings we'd seen in the Best of the Past.

While Shelby and I completed our end of day routine at Buckingham's, Lady Anthea had stayed in my office and typed, printed, and even talked to herself a little. Based on the *ohs* and *my, my*s I'd heard, it sounded like she'd been surprised several times by something or another. When I stuck my head in, she was sitting back in her chair with her hand over her mouth, looking at the computer monitor like it had talked dirty to her. I'd say she'd been stupefied by what she saw.

Now that she'd had something good to eat and drink, she was ready to report on her findings. "From my research on those paintings, I believe the two we saw to be extremely valuable," she said. She took a ladylike sip of wine while she let that sink in. "They're both unsigned, but I think they're from the school of artists like John Martin Tracy and James Henry Beard," She waited for our reaction, but we didn't react. I had never heard of either artist, so what was I supposed to say?

"Not John Martin Tracy and James Henry Beard!" Shelby shrieked. "No!"

"Have you heard of them?" I asked.

"Nope," Shelby said, and cracked up.

I laughed too, but that could have been the combination of the joke, the wine, and my fatigue. Whatever the cause, I needed it bad.

"They're both nineteenth century *American* artists," Lady Anthea said. That seemed to make the gap in our education even more shameful.

"Still not ringing any bells with me," I said.

"I need to do more research but this is what I can tell you from what I know thus far. A painting by James Henry Beard would probably cost in the five- to ten-thousand-pound range."

"Wow," I said. I didn't need to do any arithmetic on the exchange rate to know what she was saying was important.

"And, John Martin Tracy was the first famous artist to paint pointing dogs in the States," she said.

"Were his as valuable as the first guy?" Shelby asked, leaning in.

"Oh, you would have to pay much more for an oil painting by John Martin Tracy."

Dare I ask? "How much more?"

"His works sell for one hundred thousand and up."

"Not that it matters, but pounds or dollars?" I asked.

"Dollars." She'd kindly converted for us, but if the six-figure number had been anything but pennies, it would have been a lot of money.

"But you're not saying the paintings we saw at the Best of the Past were by either of them, right? Not even the less valuable one? They were from the school of, right?" Shelby asked.

"Oh, no! As far as I know, Tracy and Beard always signed their works. Those weren't signed," Lady Anthea reminded us. "At least I didn't see a signature. If I could see it unframed, who knows." She shook her head. "I would never trust myself to take it out of its frame. For now, dating the artwork will have to suffice. If they are oil paintings from the nineteenth century…" She let her voice trail off.

I thought I had gotten her drift, but I wanted to be sure. "You can't determine their value by who the artist is, because we don't know. You're going by how old they look?"

She had been nodding that I was right up until my question. "It's not how old they *look*. Any forger worth his salt can make a painting look old. There are very reliable ways to date a painting."

The leaves on the Golden Euonymus along the back property line glowed in the night, illuminating my backyard. Lady Anthea's news showed us what we didn't know and would hopefully lead us to the right questions. "Collins said those paintings were fine for a bachelor's apartment," I said. I looked at Shelby since she hadn't been there. "He gave us the distinct impression his paintings weren't valuable at all."

Lady Anthea reached for another slice. "I think they're worth much more than he was leading us to believe. I can't help but wonder why a gallery owner would be keen to undervalue his merchandise? Is that an American sales approach?"

Shelby and I shook our heads, no.

Lady Anthea said, "Let's not get ahead of ourselves. I need to do more research before I can say with any certainty how valuable his paintings are."

"How could he not know the paintings' worth?" Shelby asked. "I mean, he owns the gallery. He should know since he bought them."

"He said that Mary Jane Kerwin did the buying," Lady Anthea said.

"Yes, but remember he said he had inherited those," I corrected and had another bite. "Well, we learned that Henry bought a painting from the group—at least one." I stopped and told Shelby about the piece with the sold notice on it. "Collins said that Henry had bought it, making it his second, but Mary Jane Kerwin said Henry hadn't paid for it and took the note off." I pointed at Lady Anthea with my slice of pizza. "Is that why you wanted to get us into Henry's apartment? So we could see if the first painting was by the same artist as those in the gallery?"

She raised one eyebrow and gave a devious little chuckle.

"Good for you," Shelby said.

"I have much more to consider," Lady Anthea said.

"You were working hard on the computer this afternoon," I said. "What I don't understand is how whatever you find on the internet can tell you if a painting in front of you is the real deal."

"That's a good point. Authentication usually relies on connoisseurs. I'm far from that, but when I first saw those paintings I was struck by the composition and those colors." She paused and lowered her voice. "Those colors—I can still see those colors."

"I'm not really an art person but I have to admit, I was awe-struck by both of those paintings," I said.

"When we were finally shed of Ashley, I enlarged the photos so I could see the brushstrokes better. When we go to Henry's apartment, I'm going to look at the paint texture and the frame of the first one he bought," Lady Anthea explained.

"Is there anything you need from us?" Shelby asked.

"Not unless you have a lab for infrared spectroscopy, radiometric dating, or gas chromatography," Lady Anthea answered. When she saw the blank looks on our faces, she adjusted her request downward. "I could use the help of someone who really knows her way around the internet for provenance research," Lady Anthea said, looking first at me then at Shelby.

"Never been to France," Shelby said.

That got a raised eyebrow from Lady Anthea.

"Provenance is who owned the artwork when, right?" I asked.

"That's right. Can either of you help with the provenance online research?"

"Dana can!" we answered at the same time.

Shelby laughed. "Sure, Sue and I can google, but Dana deep dives into social media sites and groups to find the good stuff."

I knew better than to look at Shelby when she said this since the *good stuff* was mostly background on Frithsden and the duke.

Lady Anthea sank back into her chair. "I'm delighted and relieved we have access to someone like that."

After helping herself to more salad, Shelby said, "*I'm* glad we have someone like you who knows something about art. How do you know so much? Did you study art history in school?"

"Yes, and my family has a collection curated over generations," she said. The end of her sentence had trailed off. Then she shook her head like she was thinking an unpleasant thought away, and laughed. "I have to say, I have laughed more this week than I have in the past year." She picked up her wine glass to toast us. "I'm grateful to you both for that."

"Are you kidding?" I asked. "Which was more fun: finding the dead body, the car wreck...?"

Shelby interrupted me. "Baring your soul to a newspaper when that was the last thing you wanted to do? Or, wait don't tell me, was it Ashley Trent's scene this afternoon?" She had pushed back the heavyweight chair and was getting ready to head out. "Before I go, are we in agreement that the person Henry was referring to as *boss* on his calendar was Mary Jane Kerwin?"

"We know it wasn't Sue he was having sex with," Lady Anthea said, with what I thought was an uncalled for degree of certainty.

"I think we can assume it was Ms. Kerwin, but when we see his calendar entry for Sunday night, we'll know for sure. Remember, Rick Ziegler saw the van on Sunday night, the night before Henry was murdered."

Shelby left through the side door to the porch, and Lady Anthea and I brought the now-empty pizza box and salad bowl in through the door to my great room. Abby was already inside and snoozing on the hearth.

"This is a very comfortable home, Sue." She scanned the room, even though she'd seen it every day since Monday.

For some reason, I did the same. I looked over the room though it was even more than familiar to me. "I inherited every single piece of furniture in here. I had the chairs and sofa reupholstered." The sea motif might have been too busy, but having all three covered in the same fabric kept the room tranquil. The walls were painted the color of sand from an East Coast beach and the floorboards were close to white.

We put the dinner dishes in the dishwasher, and I went back to sit in one of the two chairs. Lady Anthea sunk into the overstuffed sofa, placing her phone on the cushion next to her leg.

"It's been a long day," I said, trying to cover a yawn. "I didn't sleep very well last night because I was wired after the wreck."

Her phone rang. She didn't automatically answer the call, instead she picked the phone up and looked at it. "It's my brother," she said.

This was just the excuse I needed to go to bed. "Go ahead and talk to him. Good night."

She nodded and answered the phone. I was in the middle of the room and I still heard a man's voice bellow out. "You mentioned Sandringham to a newspaper?! What are you doing over there?!"

Chapter 19

On Thursday I woke up still angry with Lady Anthea's brother for berating her the way he had. My six o'clock run on the Lewes beach was enjoyable once I stopped planning what I would say to the duke if I ever met him in person. That wasn't likely ever to occur, so he was safe from the blistering and brilliant attack I had prepared. I hadn't let on to Lady Anthea that I had heard the opening to his tirade about her speaking of Sandringham to the media because I didn't want to embarrass her. After getting ready for work I had gone to Buckingham's to open for the day. When Shelby came in, I went back home to pick Lady Anthea up for our trip to Henry's apartment.

"I hope Ashley will give us the key and leave us to go through Henry's belongings by ourselves, instead of staying with us," I said, as I clicked my seatbelt buckle.

"We would be able to communicate with each other more freely if she would," she agreed. She paused, then said, "Did you read the *Southern Delaware Daily* article?"

"It's out already?"

"Oh, yes." She sighed out the words. "My brother read it. He has alerts so he'll be notified when Frithsden is mentioned."

So that was how her brother knew she'd discussed whatever happened at Sandringham with a reporter! Of course.

"I remember on Tuesday when we saw the article with the dog theft rumor, you said that you had Google alerts set up for your estate, and for friends." Actually, she'd said, *uh, friends.*

"That's what last night's phone call was all about," she said. "He wants me to return to England in case there's any explaining needed to—" she hesitated, "to our friends."

"Friends that live in palaces?" I ventured.

She chuckled but didn't answer.

"I'm so sorry you had to get involved in this," I said.

She shrugged off my apology.

"Do you need to go back?" I asked.

"I don't want to," she answered. She waited then started talking again. "He says the business has gone all to pot. I'm sure he'll continue to pressure me to distance myself from Buckingham's until the publicity fades, and that won't happen until the murder is solved."

I drove on without speaking, and wishing she had said something more along the lines of "hell no, I won't go," but she hadn't. The call from her brother topped off my anxiety level, already high because we were a day closer to the gala. Then there was my absence from my surfboard for four days. That didn't help my spirits any.

"What else did the article say?" I asked. "Please tell me they mentioned the gala?"

"Oh yes! They went into quite a bit of detail on the event. In the middle there was a paragraph detailing how the investigation had proved there was no credence to the allegation that the dogs were the target of a kidnapping plot. Don't you find that interesting?"

"I guess, I mean the rumor was ridiculous."

"I forgot to talk to them about the rumor," she said. "I think Chief Turner was the source of the retraction."

"Nah, that was me," I said. "I told Michael that Dr. Walton was drunk when he called them."

She laughed. "I thought I had found an opportunity to put in a good word for your chief. I'll have to keep trying. They were very kind in describing the beach location and that the entertainment would be provided by a DJ along with a guitarist."

I drove on, taking on board what she was saying. We were out of the Villages of Five Points and onto Highway 1, headed north to Henry's apartment in Milford.

She waited for some kind of response from me. When it didn't come, she said, "I think you'll be quite pleased when you read it."

I took a deep lungful of air. She had gone way outside her comfort zone when she gave that interview. It was time for me to do the same and talk to her. "It's just that at the beginning of the week I was worried about getting the centerpieces just right, and keeping up with all the extra business your appearance was bringing in. The Pet Parent Appreciation Gala was supposed to help us take Buckingham's to the next level. We wanted people that used our services every other month to increase that to once a month. If we've been seeing them once a week, we wanted them booking twice a week. Now with what we've contracted to spend on food, drink, decorations, and whatever else, it'll take us a year to get out of the red."

"If we repair damage done by the murder and have a successful gala, can we keep up with increased usage of our services? We don't have a big staff," she said.

"Oh, I'd love to have enough business to hire a few more people."

"Would you hire me?" she asked.

That should have been followed by a laugh, but it wasn't. "In a heartbeat," I said.

"I feel I haven't been much help this week." Her voice was low and tentative.

"Are you kidding? Every time I turn around you're saving my backside." I looked over at her just in time to see her head jerk. Maybe I'd gotten a little too informal with that last line. "I mean—"

"I know what you mean. I've used the Anglophilia any time I thought it would help," Lady Anthea said with an unembarrassed laugh. "Seriously, what would you hire me to do?"

Though I knew this was a rhetorical question she'd gone back to, I did have an idea to throw out. "You're really good with dogs. I would love to hire someone to specialize in agility training."

"Two of my three corgis have won agility competitions."

We went back to our own thoughts. Mine had to do with how out of character these what-ifs seemed.

In a minute or so, Lady Anthea blurted out, "Why haven't the police done more to find Henry's killer?" I heard the desperation in her voice.

"I'm not trying to defend Chief Turner—you know I'm not—but he is trying," I said. "The Lewes Police Department is small."

"Do you know what I think?" Lady Anthea said.

Just like magic my phone rang, and I could see from caller ID that it was Chief Turner himself. Since I'm a person with free will, I waited for the real live person beside me to finish her thought, instead of answering the call. It was probably all in my head, but I could have sworn the ringtone's volume increased to show that this bit of defiance against technology had not gone unnoticed and would not be tolerated.

"Don't you want to answer that?" Lady Anthea asked.

I pressed the button on my steering wheel and answered. If I had it to do all over again, I would warn my passenger I was about to do that.

"I think your Chief Turner loves his technology too much!" she said.

Your?

"Too much?" he asked. He had heard her. "It's the way we investigate crimes today."

"Have you ever stopped to think that there are more effective methods to be utilized in a small village?" she demanded. "Sue has been ahead of you every step of the way in this investigation."

"I agree," he said.

"That's because people know her and talk to her."

"I said I agree with you."

"Thanks," I said. "An admission like that shouldn't go unrewarded. Wouldn't be right. Last night we found out that Ashley suspected Henry had a girlfriend here in Lewes. And by suspected, I mean she knew."

The dead air told me he was considering this new information. "So she had a motive, but thanks to *technology* we already eliminated her from the suspect pool." He exhaled and then went on. "I'll check again on the time of death. Maybe if we used the earliest limit…" He trailed off.

"You're going by where she was when you reached her. Have you tried cell tracing to see where her phone was that afternoon? Wait, come to think of it, that might not do any good," I said.

He chuckled in what has been described in many a book as a mirthless laugh. "What do you know about cell tracing? Been on the internet?"

"First, everyone is on the internet. Next, in a book I read, *Calling All Killers,* the killer left her cell phone at home and went to kill her"—here I veered from the truth—"local police chief. Gruesome. Painful."

"I called to tell you what I found out from the victim's bank. He had made a large deposit last month. That's all they would tell me, but from what you said his salary was, he didn't make that much money working overtime or fudging his expenses."

"Do you know where the money came from?" I asked.

"I have to get a warrant to get the source of the deposit and the amount," Chief Turner said. Lady Anthea and I looked at each other and tilted our heads, looking as pure as possible for women our age. The good police chief was going to learn Henry had deposited fifty-thousand dollars into his checking account.

"I should have the information this afternoon or tomorrow at the latest."

"Have you run the background check on Mary Jane Kerwin?" I asked.

"I've requested it, but it's not back yet," he said then he hung up, which was just as well. I didn't want him hearing anything in my voice.

"If we told him about Mary Jane's and Henry's matching deposits, he wouldn't be able to use the information in court," I said to my partner.

Lady Anthea rubbed her forehead. "Please don't tell me which book that was from. Not right now."

I closed my lips, tight. It was obvious I had given her too many delectable titles to remember.

Traffic was heavy on Highway 1, but we were all able to drive at or above the fifty-mile-per-hour speed limit.

"Sue, let's talk about what we're hoping to find. I wrangled getting into Henry's apartment out of Ashley because I wanted to see the painting he bought. Anything else we should look for?"

"I'd love to know where his extra money came from. She said the police had taken some things, but if there are any financial records lying around, I won't turn my face from them," I answered. "We saw Mary Jane Kerwin's big checking account deposit was made three weeks ago. And Ashley said they bought a new car and paid off some bills at about the same time. Plus, the painting he bought. Let's not forget that. Their simultaneous windfalls had to be from the same source."

"I agree. Any alternative to that would be too much of a coincidence for belief," Lady Anthea said. "We don't know how far in debt the couple were, do we?"

"Nope. Why?" I asked.

Suddenly a Lewes police cruiser, no lights or siren but driving hell bent for leather, passed us. Too fast for us to see who was driving. We couldn't help but look at it until it was out of sight.

"I was wondering if that amount of money would be enough to buy a car, along with a prized painting," she said.

"We don't know how much Henry paid for the painting. Listening to Peter Collins, it didn't sound like he had paid him very much," I said.

"Oh, he would have paid quite a bit for a nineteenth-century painting."

"When we get Dana working on researching its provenance, we'll know how much, right?" Something else was bothering me. "Why?"

"Why, what?" she asked.

"The funny thing is Henry didn't seem like the kind of person to buy a work of art. And why would he buy a painting and keep it here? Wouldn't he have taken it to his and Ashley's home?"

"How do you know he didn't?" she asked.

"Well, when Ashley was listing what they had done with the money, she didn't mention buying art. I think she would have if she knew about the painting. Maybe he was going to surprise her with it."

"Yes, maybe it was his intention to take it to New York. Ashley said he came home once a month, maybe he hadn't been home since he made the purchase," Lady Anthea said. She looked out at the scenery. "As for his reason for purchasing the painting, it could have been as an investment or aesthetics, you know their visual appeal. I saw how the two on the wall at the Best of the Past affected you."

"I wanted to walk into them," I admitted as I slowed for the light to turn off Route 1 onto Highway 16. "Do you think I felt that way because of how large they were?"

"I think it was more likely that while the focus was on the subject, the objects in the background were interesting also." We were driving past farmland, and she waved her hand toward it in an attempt to illustrate her point.

"The way one color disappeared into another was intriguing. I wanted to keep looking at them," I added. "Them," I repeated.

We stopped at the red light at a small yellow building. It was an antiques store named: A Walk Through Time. I arranged my brainwaves, then I turned to Lady Anthea. "Peter Collins said Henry had bought a second painting."

"But Mary Jane Kerwin disputed that."

"She said he hadn't paid for it. I got the impression that he intended to buy it. It sounds like he had the money for another expensive painting," I said.

"Or he had the expectation of more money," Lady Anthea added. "You're saying whatever business dealings the two of them were engaged in was ongoing?"

"Yes, and his murder ended it," I speculated as I turned right into the entrance of a subdivision of townhouses.

"Or maybe Mary Jane Kerwin will carry on without him," Lady Anthea said. "Twice the money for her. So their business partnership makes her a prime suspect, correct?"

"At least *a* suspect."

"I assumed it was a love match, with jealousy as a motive. She found out about Ashley, she killed him. But didn't she have a monetary reason for wanting Henry alive if they were about to make more money?" Lady Anthea asked.

"Maybe she was afraid he would cut her out. But out of what? What were the two of them doing to get that much money?" I gave the steering wheel a whack with both palms.

The solitary street in the development was flanked by a row of townhouses on either side. Patches of grass made a valiant attempt at survival, but bare, gray ground covered most of what wasn't paved.

"I wanted to tell Chief Turner about my suspicion that Mary Jane Kerwin and Henry knew each other before he moved here, but their deposits being made so soon after Henry's arrival is my reason for thinking that, and we can't tell him how we know what's on her bank statement. I guess we'll have to figure that out on our own."

"I thought we would be safe here," Lady Anthea said. That's when I realized this time it was she who had gotten quiet, dating from about the time we turned into Henry's neighborhood, as I had rambled on. "Aren't we in a different town?" she asked.

She was staring straight ahead, and not happy about what she saw. At the end of the street sat two police cars, grills facing. One was marked *Lewes*. The other was marked *City of Milford*. Chief Turner and a man I didn't recognized stood talking and yucking it up. If the signage on the side of his car was to be believed, and I saw no reason not to, this was the Milford police chief. Ashley's SUV was in the driveway, but I didn't see her.

"All I have to remember is we don't know about Ms. Kerwin's deposit. Right?" Lady Anthea asked.

"Right. We never saw Mary Jane Kerwin's bank statement," I said, hardly moving my lips.

"And it's not in my handbag."

Chapter 20

"Sue Patrick, good morning." Chief Turner's tone wished me anything but a good morning. He turned to Lady Anthea, and she was the next recipient of what she might characterize as his cheeky attitude. This far into the week we were immune to it, but it seemed too much for the Milford police chief to handle and he stood down. He gave Chief Turner a nod and headed for the safety of his car.

"See you later, George." Turner turned to me and sighed. "You two are here. I'm here. What a coincidence."

I rolled my eyes to show him that I knew there was nothing coincidental about this meeting. He had been driving the police car that had blown by us. In my peripheral vision, I saw Lady Anthea watching the retreating back of the other police chief. She cocked her head to the right and left, like Abby does when she's processing unfamiliar words.

"What did you say to annoy him?" I asked.

"He met me here as a professional courtesy. Since this isn't my jurisdiction I called him before I drove over. Again, professional courtesy. You see, we, unlike you two, are *professionals*."

"And courteous?" I said.

He chuckled. "When I want to be I…"

I didn't wait for him to finish. "Why are you here? You already searched Henry's home."

"Why are you two here?" he asked.

"Just visiting Ashley." I was a little embarrassed at how stupid that lie was, and my heart wasn't into it.

"And what were you doing at that antiques store yesterday? I doubt you were shopping."

"We could have been," I said.

"You went there to talk to Mary Jane Kerwin. I won't ask how you found out she was the girlfriend. I don't want to know." He turned to Lady Anthea. "See, I'm taking your advice and availing myself of what people confide in Sue." Then he looked back at me. "Just tell me this. Did Mary Jane Kerwin know she wasn't the only woman in Henry Cannon's life?"

"She knew about Ashley," I answered.

Lady Anthea added, "She said she ended it when she learned about Ashley, but I'm not sure she's to be believed."

"So both women could be on our suspect list," he said.

"Our?" He had to have known I would jump on that.

"I misspoke. *My* suspect list." In spite of himself, he almost laughed, then he looked out at the distance. "Since the victim had been drugged with sleeping pills, a smaller person could have overpowered him." He looked back at me. "By the way, a quarter of the town takes those pills."

I looked at the ground because I don't trust myself to have a poker face, and I wasn't about to lead him to Dayle Thomas, as ill as she was.

"I don't mind admitting my money was on the veterinarian as the murderer, but I don't have anything else incriminating Walton," he said. He hesitated and gave me a closer inspection. "Sue, you got quiet all of a sudden. Wait, do you take sleeping pills?"

I jerked my head up. "Me? No! I work hard and I spend as much time as I can in the ocean."

Chief Turner grinned and then retreated to his usual serious self. "We searched Dr. Walton's house. We even took a canine unit—"

"A canine unit? And you didn't freak?" I interrupted.

"Very funny. By the way, the handler said to tell you hi. We didn't find the shirt or the knife on the premises. The vet seems to be the only person in town who doesn't tell me you walk on water. I keep thinking there's something I'm missing about that guy. If he dislikes you enough to want to run you off the road and down an embankment, you gotta figure he could be your employee's murderer."

His phone rang and he looked at the screen, and then quickly turned away from us and answered it. Lady Anthea and I took that opportunity to go inside Henry's former home.

"Why were you looking at the Milford police chief like that?" I asked.

"When I was at university, we learned about a nineteenth-century artist who didn't sign his paintings. His favorite subject was dogs. I couldn't sleep last night after my brother called, and I stayed awake trying to remember the name." She stopped and looked back at the street. "I think the first name was George, the same as that gentleman."

"Pricey?" I asked.

"Extremely."

The door was unlocked. In the living room Ashley was sitting on a black leather loveseat, with her elbows propped on her knees and her head buried in her hands.

"Ashley?" Lady Anthea called soothingly. We walked over, and Anthea sat beside her and rubbed her shoulders.

Ashley looked up. "I don't know what to do with this all this stuff." She swung her arm around to indicate the living room.

Honestly, there wasn't that much. It was pretty sparsely furnished. "What do you *want* to do with it?" I asked. It's always amazed me at how seldom people ask themselves that question. What do I really want right now?

Ashley looked down at the loveseat. "I don't want to move this furniture back to Albany."

"I can recommend a charity that will come pick it up," I said.

She looked up at me. "Well, okay."

Lady Anthea gave Ashley's back a final pat and stood. "Just tell us which items you wish to donate."

I opened a note app on my phone and typed in *loveseat*.

"Let's walk around," Lady Anthea said.

In my head, I heard a fiddle. The one my business partner was once again playing Ashley like. This was how we would search the apartment and find the painting. What would Lady Anthea say to keep her from including it with the items to go to charity when we came to it? I couldn't wait to hear. Though Henry didn't deserve to be murdered, he and Ashley certainly deserved each other. I was completely convinced of that. Neither was as smart as they thought.

Ashley led Lady Anthea in a slow walk around the perimeter of the room, as if we couldn't see the whole space from the loveseat. I followed behind them making notes like an earnest girl reporter. *R-u-u-u-ug*, I typed and tried not to roll my eyes. The eat-in kitchen was furnished with a café table and two cheap-o chairs. A small metal desk sat in the corner, which had one file-size drawer and one junk drawer.

Suddenly Ashley turned around to me. "Why don't you look for the information we talked about last night?" She emphasized *last night,* like it was a code.

I hesitated a beat because I had no idea what she was talking about until I recalled that we were supposed to be looking for something that would tell us who Henry was cheating on her with. I think she was trying to telegraph to me that I wasn't 100 percent off her suspect list.

I nodded and sat at the desk. If you think looking at someone's cheap-ass furniture is boring, try looking for information you already know. It seemed like I'd known who Henry's local girlfriend was most of my life. I reminded myself that I was really looking to see where Henry's big bucks had come from, but it was hard not to shoot up off the chair and yell, "I found out it wasn't me. Whew!" Or maybe, "Eureka! Mary Jane Kerwin!"

After ascertaining that Henry's china was of the paper variety, and that his glassware could best be described as red Solo cups, Ashley invited Lady Anthea upstairs to the loft bedroom. "Yesterday I packed all his clothes in boxes, and I checked the pockets." She looked over Lady Anthea's shoulder at me. "For restaurant receipts," she hissed. Then she turned on her heel to go upstairs.

I opened what turned out to be a junk drawer and started going through takeout menus. I needed to get myself really bored or I was going to start laughing.

Lady Anthea came back down in less than five minutes. "I suggested to her that some alone time might be what she needed."

"You're a real humanitarian, you know that? You found out what you wanted to know and then you couldn't wait to get away from her, right?" I asked, under my breath.

She looked up at the loft to be sure we weren't being watched, then nodded. "It's not here."

"What's not?"

"I swear, Chief Turner, somebody ought to put a bell on you!" I said as loud as I dared. "None of your business."

"Why don't you let me be the judge of that?" he asked, though I doubted it was really a question.

Lady Anthea stepped forward and in a low voice said, "Why don't the two of you go outside to discuss this?" She jerked her head to the floor above us where Ashley was rummaging.

"Ladies first," he said and followed me to the front door.

We stood by his car and I told him a decent percent of what I knew: that Henry had purchased a painting from the Best of the Past and that he and Mary Jane Kerwin had told the owner, Peter Collins, that it was pretty much as valuable as a painting of Elvis on black velvet, when in fact it was worth tens of thousands of dollars and or pounds, I couldn't remember which.

"We thought we would find the painting here, but now we don't know where it is," I said to wrap it up.

He stared at me with his mouth open, the way some cats behold certain shows on Animal Planet. "So that's the real reason you and Lady Anthea are here at the victim's home?"

"Yeah, would I lie to you?"

He closed his eyes and shook his head. "Have you asked Ashley where it is?"

"Um, no."

"Then what reason did you give her for coming here? And going through her fiancé's personal belongings?"

I sighed in exasperation at having to go into that sensitive area. "She thinks I was Henry's girlfriend and—"

His laugh was explosive, and at first I thought he was choking.

"What's so funny?"

"I never met the guy and I know he was not the man for you," he said, his voice lowering with each word. He spoke with a familiarity bordering on unearned intimacy.

"You don't know me at all," I said and walked to get in my Jeep.

"That's true." He had followed me, practically on my heels, like a young terrier. "I just meant, I don't see him being your type. That's all."

"I don't date my employees and I don't date dead guys." I got in and slammed the door, which unfortunately doesn't have the level of drama in a Jeep that it does in a car with heftier doors. I wanted to leave but that would mean stranding my partner. Chief Turner raised his hand to knock on the window and realized there wasn't one.

"Would you turn around?"

"Huh?" he asked.

"Please. I have to get this calendar out of my pants. It hurts."

After a startled look, he did as asked. I lifted my shirt and pulled the cardboard twelve-page, not counting the front and back covers, offending item out of my waistband. "You can turn back around now."

I held up the calendar. "Henry used to write his scheduled times to see Mary Jane in here. At least that's who we were assuming he was going to meet."

He pointed to the Rick Ziegler's Raw-k & Roll logo on the cover. "A freebie?"

"Yeah, to Henry and me." I opened it to last Sunday. "We know he saw Mary Jane Kerwin Sunday night. And here it is. *Boss* is written on Sunday and Monday." Henry had written *late* by both. "That's proof that he referred to Mary Jane Kerwin as boss."

"We already knew she was his local bit on the side. How does this help us?"

"According to Ashley, in his checkbook he wrote *Boss* by the large deposit."

"So he was getting money from her? In addition to, well, you know... Thank you for the information."

"Are you going to question Mary Jane Kerwin?" I asked without looking at him. Lady Anthea had come out, alone, and was headed for the car.

"Yes, I'll bring her in," he said.

"I wonder if the painting is at her house," I said. "Maybe Henry bought it as a gift for her."

"Could that painting be valuable enough for someone to have killed him to get their hands on it?" he asked.

I pointed at Lady Anthea and said, "She's still researching it, but it looks like it."

"I need to know if it's missing," he said.

Rather than walking to the passenger side of the Jeep and getting in, she walked up to Chief Turner.

"Chief?" Lady Anthea called to him. When she had his attention, she lowered first one eyebrow then the boom. "Tracking her mobile phone is not winning points. She and I are on our way back to Buckingham's." She had spoken in a whisper, but she was standing close by, and I would have heard even if I didn't have ears like a dog.

"*She* is sitting right here," I said.

He sputtered, looked down, took off his cap, and rubbed his hand over his head, all while Lady Anthea calmly went around to the other side of the Jeep and got in.

"Look," Chief Turner said, "I'll go back in and ask Ashley if Henry brought any expensive purchases home to Albany. Neither of you said anything to Ms. Trent about a painting, right?"

We both shook our heads, no.

My phone rang and I saw it was Buckingham's. Since I didn't know the subject of the call I pulled onto the road and left Chief Turner standing there. Just in case.

"Sue, you didn't find the painting, did you?" Shelby asked.

"No, we didn't. Maybe it's in Mary Jane Kerwin's house. Or it could already be in Albany, though Ashley didn't mention it. How did you know?" I asked.

"I'll put Dana on since she deserves all the credit."

"Sue, it's Dana," a young, eager voice said.

"Hi, kiddo," I answered.

"I have some information for you," she said.

"Did you find out how much Henry paid for the painting?" Lady Anthea asked. She was leaning forward to the speaker.

"I found out something much more important. He sold it to a gallery in New York."

Chapter 21

Lady Anthea and I used the rest of the drive back to Buckingham's rearranging the cart and the horse, and generally smacking our heads with our palms.

"All along we assumed Henry and Mary Jane came into money—" she said.

I interrupted, "Probably from corrupt means since he lied to his fiancée when he told her it was from his job at the Pet Palace. After all, if it was on the up and up, why not tell Ashley the truth?"

She nodded her head as fast as it would go. "When the truth was, he paid Peter Collins a pittance for the paintings." She stopped to smirk at her sarcastic tongue twister.

I took my mind off the murder to think about how funny she thought her lame jokes were. I wanted to think that as long as you enjoyed your own humor, that was all that mattered, but even I wasn't that open-minded.

"Then he and Mary Jane divided the profits," she continued. She seemed to feel the need to steel herself for the next part and took a deep breath. "I feel we should apprise Chief Turner of this new development."

I looked over and she was biting her lower lip.

"Okay," I said. "He needs to know that the killer didn't steal the painting from Henry."

She exhaled a *whew*.

"The clock is ticking, what with your brother breathing down your neck and the gala being tomorrow night. I agree with you completely that we should tell him where Henry's money was coming from. I'll get him on the phone right now."

"I was afraid you might not want to because of this competition you and he seem to fall into," she said.

"I want the investigation to move faster, and to put it kindly, he's methodical."

"Methodical is generous. He plods. At least he agreed to use your contacts in town when he needs them," she reminded me.

"Oh, I won't hold my breath until he asks me for help."

I was about to place the call to Chief Turner, but stopped again. "It was Peter Collins they were cheating. Shouldn't he be on the suspect list?" I asked.

"He was in New York that day."

"No one has confirmed that," I said.

"He's only a suspect if he knew he was being cheated," she countered.

"Okay, let's give all this to Chief Turner." I found his number in my recent call list and told my car to phone him.

"Suuuuuue!" He bellowed.

I hung up.

My phone rang before we had driven a mile and not being petty, I answered it.

"Did you just hang up on me?" Chief Turner asked.

"No," I said.

"Whatever. Did you know that Mary Jane Kerwin came into a large amount of money at the same time as Henry? Is that why you asked me to run a background check on her?"

"You have the results?" Lady Anthea asked in a masterful stroke of diversion.

"She was licensed as a registered nurse. Received her training right here in Lewes at Beebe." His cadence was measured and he was doing a low boil.

"She was licensed as a R.N.? Past tense?" I asked.

"She was under review when she left, uh, where she used to work."

"Hold on," I interrupted. He knew where she had worked as an R.N. and he knew I knew that he knew. There was only one reason he wouldn't want to tell me where that was.

He laughed, knowing he'd let the cat out of the bag.

"She worked in a hospital in Albany?" I offered. When would the guy learn he couldn't elude my rapidly advancing detecting abilities? Sure, I'd only learned this week that I had a super power, but I'd been unconsciously honing it for years. Like the amateur sleuth in *Sharp Knives and Dull Neighbors.*

"Yeah, the hospital she worked for was in Albany, New York. The official reason for her departure from the hospital was something innocuous, but a call by a friend of a friend with the Albany P.D. came up with something more interesting." He paused and for a beat I thought he was going to make me ask him, forfeiting my respect. I was glad when it turned out he was getting a swig of coffee. I had wondered if such a deep speaking voice required extra hydration. "After the second time she was added to a wealthy patient's will and the family threatened to bring charges, as well as cut off their donations to the hospital foundation, she was asked to resign. Management didn't know how she was doing what she was doing, and they didn't want to know. They didn't want her doing it on their premises."

"So, it's likely she and Henry met in Albany," I said.

"Good guess," Chief Turner said. "I'm on my way to her house now. Having a female officer meet me there."

"Good idea. A man's got to know his own limitations," I said.

He chuckled. It made me happy to hear him relax, though I didn't know why. "A man's got to recognize, t-r-o-u-b-l-e, when he sees it," he said.

"For someone not in the Elvis army you seem to know a lot of his songs," I said.

I remembered the way Mary Jane had looked at him and rubbed against him at the Best of the Past. Our chief was no dummy. "Smart," I said. An idea occurred to me. "Hey, maybe sometime I could escort you."

"No." No mistaking his meaning, but we'd see. "She's not the first person I've come upon who would do anything to get what she wanted," he said. There it was again, that something in his voice. He was tired. "I'm also having someone do a quick search of her house if she'll let us without a warrant. Before I hang up, what else have you learned that you're not telling me?"

I nodded at Lady Anthea, and she told him what we'd learned from Dana's research. If I told him we'd called him to do just that, it would have been such a letdown for the guy. We had eliminated the someone-killed-him-to-get-the-painting blind alley.

Chapter 22

Once we got back to Buckingham's, we split up into teams. Dana walked Lady Anthea through her research. They sat on the couch in my office, heads tilted together over Dana's computer tablet. Abby was perched next to Dana.

Shelby handled the front desk, with Mason stepping in when her line grew to more than two pet parents. Our other groomer, Joey, finished up the clients getting washed, dried, curled, bandana'd for tomorrow night's gala.

I sat behind my desk and reached for Henry's file. It wasn't on the corner of my desk where I'd left it yesterday afternoon.

I went back to reception and waited for Shelby to finish with her pet parent. "Do you have Henry's file?" I whispered. "I can't find it."

"I hid it from Ashley yesterday. It's in the bottom drawer of your file cabinet."

"Smart move," I said.

"I wasn't fast enough. By the time I'd chased her into your office, she had picked it up and was reading it."

"So that's how she knew where Chief Turner's misinformation about her being Henry's sister came from," I said.

I returned to my office and woke my computer up. I told Dana and Lady Anthea about Ashley looking at Henry's personnel file, then they went back to talking in serious, low tones. Finally, Lady Anthea said, "Dana found the missing painting. Another beautiful work of art."

"We've never seen Henry's painting. How do you know that's it?" I asked.

Both Dana and Lady Anthea looked at me with pity. Lady Anthea took on the onerous task of educating me. "Dana has reconstructed the painting's trail from the Collins family to Henry to a Manhattan art dealer to the buyer. That's how we know. And, every step was legal. The others—the two we saw at the antique gallery—are still with the family."

Mason stuck his head in the door to my office. "Can I take Abby to be groomed now? I've been trying to get her in since Monday."

"Sure. Thanks." I turned to Abby, still sitting on the sofa, intelligently following the conversation on the buying and selling of fine art. "Want to go with Mason, girl?"

Mason bowed at Lady Anthea, then squeezed in beside her. I saw her eyes widen in surprise but she didn't say anything.

Mason, however, did. "Laliberte!" He pointed at the screen of the tablet.

Every eye in the room was on him, even Abby's beautiful brown globes.

"Well?" Mason asked the room. "I'm right, aren't I? Isn't that painting by Laliberte?"

"Yes," Lady Anthea said. "Are you familiar with him?"

"No-o-o-o. I'm familiar with *her*," he said.

"That explains—well, everything," Lady Anthea said. She was still looking at Mason in wonderment.

"Speak for yourself," I said.

Lady Anthea stood and began pacing. "Very few fine art academies admitted women until the mid-1800s. The education would have been incomplete without drawing a nude, which was not allowed. Add to that the fact that those wealthy enough to have their portraits painted refused to hire women artists, and you'll see how difficult it was a woman to display and sell her art under her own name at the time, even if she was self-taught." She stopped and turned back to Mason. "These unsigned paintings were by a woman. How did you know this painting was by her?"

"Sure, it is," he said. "Look." He flicked his fingers on the screen to enlarge a section and then pointed at the hunting dog's straight back.

Lady Anthea returned to the sofa and I joined her.

"Can you see it?" Mason asked.

"There it is!" Dana squealed.

"I'll be damned," I said. The dog's fur curled into lettering, and it seemed to happen as I watched. L-A-L-I-B-E-R-T-E.

"I'm gobsmacked." Lady Anthea watched as Mason bounded up from the sofa.

"Come on, Abby, let's go," he said. Then he slapped the side of his leg, and Abby jumped down and stood next to him, with her big brown eyes gazing up at Mason with adoration.

"How did you know that?" Lady Anthea asked.

"Ask me no questions, and I'll tell you no lies," he said on his way out with Abby.

After he was out of earshot Lady Anthea looked at me for a translation.

"Mason has a complicated love life," I said and left it at that.

"Dana, how did you find the painting without knowing the name of the artist?" I asked.

"I searched online databases using the Collins family name, the subject of the painting, and nineteenth century. The two paintings at the Best of the Past had a dog in them, so I put that in as a key word and got lucky."

Dana got up to go, and I congratulated her on a job well done.

"I liked doing it," she beamed. "I'll go relieve the daycare counselors for their breaks, but let me know if anything else comes up." She handed Lady Anthea the computer tablet. "I think I'd like to major in something like this in college."

"Information technology?" I offered.

"No, catching murderers," she said, leaving me wondering about the ethics of a boss asking a teenage employee not to mention something to her protective mother.

Lady Anthea interrupted my existential quest with an observation. "I think it's great that a painting by a woman is fetching that much in the art market."

Dana was almost at the door when she turned around. "I should check for other paintings by Laliberte to see how much they went for."

She picked up the tablet and tapped away. "Hmm. There's another Laliberte in Lewes."

"Delaware or England?" Lady Anthea asked.

"Delaware, and it's right around the corner. Dr. Walton has one. Later," she said.

Chapter 23

I opened Google Earth on my laptop and put Henry's personnel file next to it. He had worked at a veterinary clinic in Albany. I found the address and switched to a satellite view. I zoomed out and I didn't have to go far.

"Look at this," I said, motioning for Lady Anthea to come over. "It's a hospital. See how close it is to where Henry worked? How much do you want to bet they met in the neighborhood where they both worked?"

"I'd wager they met at lunch or in a coffee shop," Lady Anthea said. "Wait, do we know she worked at the hospital at the same time he worked in the veterinary clinic?"

"No," I said.

"Nor do we know the nature of their relationship at the time."

My desk phone was ringing. Before picking up, I said, "I think from the way they were abusing our poor van, we can make a pretty good guess."

The phone rang again, and I answered.

"You might want to get that. It's Shelby trying to warn you I'm here," said the deep voice. Chief Turner was standing in the doorway.

Lady Anthea jumped, grabbing her pearl choker.

"Thanks for trying, Shelby," I said and hung up.

"I have to get to the station. Mary Jane Kerwin is coming in to give a signed statement. I wanted to stop by here first," he said.

"She confessed?" Lady Anthea gasped.

I knew in my bones that wasn't what he was here to tell me, so I felt the letdown a beat earlier. That woman was tough and wasn't about to burst into tears and tell all like the end of a *Murder She Wrote* episode.

Chief Turner shook his head, no. "I bet she will soon. I have something almost as good to tell you. We found Henry's shirt and knife in the drain to her outdoor shower."

"That's where she hid it! It has to be her. She wanted the money from the sale of the next painting all for herself," Lady Anthea said, clasping her hands together. "She had to know that after you discovered she and Henry knew one another, you would learn about their dodgy business dealings."

"It would have been put in there in the last twenty-four hours." Had I just said that out loud? Lady Anthea and Chief Turner's heads pivoted to me. I had.

"How would you know that?" Chief Turner was no longer standing in the doorway. He was closing the distance between us.

"I was there yesterday and I saw her outdoor shower. It was draining fine," I said.

"Now you're a plumber?" he asked.

Lady Anthea was making a sound like she wanted to interrupt, but I plowed on. "Can we talk about this later?" By later I meant never.

He looked at his watch, then spun around and was gone.

Lady Anthea took a deep breath and returned to the sofa. After we heard the doors swish open, then closed, she said, "I remember now. When you accidently turned the water on, it didn't pool around our shoes, did it?"

"No, it drained just fine."

"Why did you make it sound like you were alone in that woman's shower stall? You didn't have to do that," Lady Anthea said.

"I think I did. I know your real life is in England. Any day now you might need to go back to salvage that life." I pointed to the door. "He might be able to stop you from leaving the country if you get any more mixed up in this murder."

She looked over my shoulder out the window behind me. The play area on that side of the building was rarely used, but we had it if it was needed. Which it hadn't been since Monday.

"Remember when I asked you why Americans did unnecessary things?" she asked.

"Like putting pumpkin flavor in coffee?" I offered.

"And you said it was because you could. Why do people have outdoor showers? Just pick up the garden hose if you need to wash sand off your feet, for heaven's sake. Are they used?"

"Both Mary Jane Kerwin and Dayle Thomas live within walking distance of the bay. They probably do use theirs after walking on the beach," I said.

She sighed. "Hopefully, Chief Turner will be able to charge Ms. Kerwin with the murder after he interrogates her. It wasn't a coincidence that after we talked to her the T-shirt and knife appeared in the drain of her shower." She rubbed her forehead, back and forth. "We've learned a lot since Monday night. I have to believe we are extremely close to figuring this out. Now, hopefully, the police will have a spot of luck and Mary Jane Kerwin will be arrested this afternoon."

"What if it wasn't her?" I asked.

Lady Anthea groaned.

"We've been disappointed before. Remember, Dr. Walton? All three of us were sure he would be charged," I said. "She had a good thing going."

"Yes, it was quite lucrative and I think she was afraid Ashley might become Henry's new business partner."

My phone pinged that I had a text. "This is from Chief Turner." I read the message: *She's lawyering up. Says somebody put the shirt in drain to frame her & full day of security footage will show her at gallery. May not be able to bring charges YET.*

I put the phone down. "Remember she said she usually worked afternoons but since Collins was away she had come in early? Now she says she was there all day."

"I was so sure this was going to be the end of it," Lady Anthea said.

"Let's list what we know," I said. "First, let's get Shelby in here."

The lobby sounded quiet, and Dana was still behind the counter, so I went out and requested Shelby's presence.

She came in and sat on the sofa next to Lady Anthea. I paced the length of my office in the style of Hercule Poirot. It got his little gray cells going. Maybe it would do the same for me. "Mary Jane Kerwin is saying the store's security cameras are going to prove she was at the Best of the Past most of the day on Monday. Chief Turner's going to need more on her to place her under arrest. We were about to run down what we've learned so far. Tell us what we're missing."

"I'm ready. Fire away," Shelby said.

"Henry dropped Dottie off. Someone stole Dayle's sleeping pills and put them in Henry's water bottle."

"Are we 100 percent sure Dayle didn't poison him herself?" Lady Anthea asked.

"What motive would she have? And why would she mention the missing sleeping pills at all if she killed him?" I asked. She nodded and I went on. "Dayle Thomas was getting chemo Monday afternoon. The person who stole the sleeping pills broke into her house, which would not have been difficult since she left her door unlocked."

I looked over to see a slight smile on Lady Anthea's face, prompting me to ask, "Do you leave the doors at Frithsden open?"

"We lock them now," she said with a smile that told me she was reminiscing. "My parents had a number of live-in servants when I was a girl and so the doors were only locked at night. I have never felt as safe as I did then. I was constantly surrounded by people who knew me."

I paused and then got back to our timeline. "Henry climbed into the back of the van, where he was stabbed," I said. I replayed in my head the way his body had looked. "His shoes were spotless. He wasn't killed somewhere else then dragged to the van. That tracks with what Chief Turner said about where the stabbing took place. But where?" I asked anyone and everyone. "Where was the van when Henry climbed into the back?"

Lady Anthea and Shelby looked at me like it had been a rhetorical question, but it hadn't been.

When Shelby realized I didn't have an answer, she spoke. "We know the van had been at the Roosevelt Inlet, but the gravel in the tires probably got there during their adult-only fun and games."

I returned to my desk and opened my notebook. "I'll list that as our first unknown—where was the van?"

Lady Anthea took the story from there. "We know that Ashley Trent, fiancée and girlfriend number one, suspected he was dating someone here. Mary Jane Kerwin, girlfriend number two, had just learned about Ashley. She and Henry knew each other in Albany. I think we can safely say she asked him to come to Lewes since they immediately started cheating her boss. They paid him a small amount for a very valuable painting, then sold it."

"Wouldn't Peter Collins be a suspect, since he was the one being cheated?" I asked.

"Remember, we considered that. We don't know if he was aware he was being defrauded. Plus, he has an alibi," Lady Anthea said.

"Mary Jane Kerwin seems like the kind of person who would want the whole pie, not half," Shelby said.

"She could have dispatched poor Henry, driven the van to the line of cars queued for the ferry, and walked home," Lady Anthea said. She stopped speaking and pointed at me. "Along the beach, like you said. She has an outdoor shower that she uses after she returns home from the beach."

"Uh-huh," I said

"Henry would get in the back of the van for her," Shelby said. "From what Rick said, and from his email to Henry, it sounded like it was a common occurrence."

The three of us looked at each other, we had all covered our mouths with our hands.

"Is it just me, or are you two thinking about them having sex in between the dog crates, with So-Long, Robber, and Paris watching?" I asked, incredulous. "It's a good thing dogs can't talk! Can you imagine So-Long reporting that to Charles Andrews?"

"That's just *wrong*," Shelby said.

"I should say so," Lady Anthea said, her disgust evident.

"Wait," I said. "It is wrong. Remember the amount of sleeping pills Henry had in his system? He wouldn't be able to perform, would he?"

"But he would still get in the back of the van for her, I'm sure," Shelby insisted.

Lady Anthea nodded in agreement. "I doubt anyone is trying to frame her."

"That's a little too pat, isn't it?" I asked.

Lady Anthea continued, "From what I saw of her, it's much more likely that she killed Henry because she was afraid he was going to stop their business arrangement or because she wanted all the money. Then she hid the shirt and knife in her drain before the police could get there."

I saw how it could have happened, step by step, just like Lady Anthea had laid out. My phone rang and I jumped out of my chair. "Hello, Chief Turner."

"Do you want to hear the latest?" he asked.

"Yeah," I said. "I'm with Shelby and Lady Anthea. I'll put you on speaker."

"I was able to get a search warrant and a crime scene team is heading over from Wilmington. We'll be looking for blood traces inside the house. That should knock her claim that someone else put the shirt and knife there out of the water. That's the good news."

He could have stopped right before that last sentence.

"What's the bad?"

"The knife doesn't match the set in her kitchen. Do people have knives that don't match?" he asked.

I looked at my fellow investigators.

"Sure," Shelby said.

"We all have one offs," Lady Anthea said.

"So the bad news wasn't so bad. The knife could still belong to her. Is that Lady Anthea I hear?" he asked.

"Yes, I'm here."

"She swears up and down that you're wrong about the paintings at the Best of the Past being valuable. Are you sure of that?"

She drew herself up in indignation. "I most certainly am."

"Good. That's what I thought. She's blaming being brought in for questioning on you."

"Don't take our word for it. We can send you the information on what the first painting sold for. I'll have Dana email it to you. She found it on the internet," I said.

"Technology saves the day again," he gloated. "We should be able to get the fingerprints off the knife in a day or so. I'll be in touch," Chief Turner said and was gone.

"A day or so will be too late. The gala is tomorrow night!" Lady Anthea said toward the phone.

"He already hung up," Shelby said, giving her shoulder a pat. "You're right, it very well could be too late. We have some pet parents, like Betsy Rivard and Dayle Thomas, saying they will definitely be there, but we have way too many still thinking about it. People who a lot of others take their cue from, like Charles Andrews and Kate Carter. Tomorrow night could go either way."

This was the first time Shelby had voiced her frustration. I shouldn't have been surprised since Jeffrey and most of their friends came from the finance world. They had lived in a condo on Wall Street. She had profit versus loss, good investment versus bad investment in her DNA.

"If, however, the killer was arrested in time for the story to make the online version of the newspaper, we'd be back to our original attendance level," Shelby continued.

Lady Anthea creased her brow. "Because people would feel safer with the killer behind bars?"

Shelby and I laughed. "Nah," I said. "They would want to come and talk about it."

As I sat there, I became aware of a tugging feeling, like Shelby and Lady Anthea and I needed to get back to what we had been talking about. I could almost feel the pull. I closed my eyes and pretended I was on my surfboard. Where was the tide taking me? My eyes shot open. "Dogs watching," I whispered. They were looking at me. "Dottie knew the person who stole Dayle's sleeping pills."

"That's right!" Shelby said. "How did anyone break in if she has a dog? After all, a Dalmatian isn't a small dog. Wait, maybe the pills were stolen before Dottie was dropped off?"

"Then how could they have been put in Henry's water bottle? If Dottie wasn't there, then Henry and his water bottle wouldn't be either. Whoever stole those pills knew Dottie and could come in the house without being bitten," I said.

"And knew the house well enough to find the pills," Lady Anthea said. "Currently that is a very confusing house." She turned to Shelby. "She's renovating."

"If we can get Mary Jane Kerwin in to Dayle's house, we'll know if she's been in it before," I said. "We can check Dottie's reaction to her too."

"How?" Shelby and Lady Anthea asked at the same time.

"Mary Jane complained about people asking her for medical advice when they learned she was a nurse. Remember how Monday's chemo treatment wiped Dayle out? Why don't I ask Mary Jane to come to Dayle's house and check on her?" I suggested.

"Sue, why would she do that?" Lady Anthea asked. "You're not exactly her favorite person."

Shelby seconded this. "She thinks—no offense, but rightly so—that you snitched on her to the police."

I looked at Lady Anthea and smiled. "Sounds like compared to you I'm pure as the driven snow. Someone with your knowledge of art wrecks what she and Henry were doing with Peter Collins's art collection. Let's call her in the morning."

My phone vibrated on my desk. "Maybe this is John texting us with an update."

"John, is it?" Lady Anthea said. "Hmm."

"It's Red. He has someone for me to sing a duet with." I typed and spoke at the same time. *Better not be an Elvis impersonator.*

I hit send and we waited.

"I feel better knowing we have a plan to get hard evidence," Lady Anthea said.

"We need someone to make a mistake. I mean, someone other than ourselves," I said for clarity.

Soon I received Red's answer: *A singer who sounds like Elvis.*

"I smell a rat," I said.

"Do you know what you'll sing?" Shelby asked.

"He hasn't said, but Elvis didn't record many duets. There was 'In the Ghetto' with Lisa Marie, but that wouldn't hit the right note for a gala, would it?"

Chapter 24

I wake up before dawn most mornings, and I was up before the sun on Friday, but when I looked at my phone, I saw I had slept an extra fifteen minutes. From what I could tell, horizontally and from the vantage point of my bed, the weather was all I could ever dream of for our Pet Parent Appreciation Gala. It was forecasted to stay that way. I rolled over and put my feet on the carpet. Nobody ever caught a killer by sleeping late, or as Lady Anthea would say, "having a lie in." Actually, I just made that up. Someone, somewhere may have.

A quick call to Dayle Thomas last night was all it had taken to get Lady Anthea and myself invited over. We told her our plan, and she sounded excited for her house and dog to play a role in the adventure. Her words had been, "If it's not cancer-related, count me in."

Five minutes later I was dressed and carrying my running shoes to the front door. I heard a smacking sound and froze. I looked around the empty family room. Who or what had made that noise?

"Yeeeessss."

Now they were whispering?

"You're a big boy, aren't you?"

That's when I caught the British accent. It was Lady Anthea. Who was the big boy? Her bedroom door was closed. I waited for her to say more, or for Big Boy to say something. I didn't have to wait long.

"Will that be all, ma'am?" The voice was male and very British. As in, ma'am sounded like mom.

Would that be all? How much had there been?

"Brilliant," Lady Anthea said. "How are their appetites?"

"Antony and Cleo are doing fine. It is only Caesar who seems despondent." Those were the names of her Corgis! "Should we plan on using Skype again tomorrow?"

"We may as well. They're rather used to it now, aren't they?"

I tiptoed away. So that's what she's been doing these mornings while I thought she was having a *lie in*. Before I got far, I heard the male voice again.

"Do you have a date for your return, ma'am?"

"I— I don't know yet," Lady Anthea answered. "Did my brother update you on what's happened here?"

"I read the article online," he said. From his tone I deduced he was a little ashamed of reading like that. Like *online* was for the wrong sort of people.

"If our efforts don't go well today, I may need to stay longer and help out. The owner is an extremely competent business woman. I'm afraid if tonight's celebration is not a success, she'll be devastated. And, as you know, Frithsden depends on the earnings from the enterprise."

I couldn't listen anymore. I left as quietly as I could, sitting on one of the front porch rocking chairs to put my running shoes on. How did I become responsible for Frithsden or for her? That's not what I wanted.

I jogged through the subdivision and passed Buckingham's. I hadn't bothered to warm up and was going faster than I intended by the time I reached Savannah Road, but I didn't care. That would be the mantra for my run. *I don't care.* How had I become so encumbered? I never asked these people to attach themselves to me. I had worked myself into quite a state when I heard the siren come on and then just as quickly die out. I stopped and bent over with my hands on my knees to look at the police car that had pulled up. Wayne's handsome face grinned out at me.

"Do you know how fast you were going, young lady?" He got out and leaned back against the side of the car, arms folded against his muscular chest. He was in his Delaware River and Bay Authority Police Uniform, but he'd left his cap in the car. "I can let you off with a warning, but only this once."

I laughed and tried to catch my breath enough to talk.

"You're crying," he said.

"No, I'm not."

He reached over and rubbed my cheek. "Then what's this?"

As we looked at the water on his fingertip, his attention was diverted by a car going by. It was a Lewes Police Department cruiser.

"There goes Chief Turner," he said with a jerk of his head. "I guess he's going home for a shower. The guy works all the time." He looked back at me. "Tonight's the big shindig?"

"Yeah, can you come?"

He looked up at the still dark sky. "Are you having anything good to eat?"

Sure, some might feel it distasteful for him to ask about food while I was crying, but not me. I thought, *bless him for not making me talk about the slight meltdown.*

"Yeah, the caterers have done a great job on the food choices," I said. "We're having heavy hors d'oeuvres."

"What do you mean, like a fifty-pound cheese ball?"

I did crack up at that. "I've got to finish my run." I turned to go, and I was laughing at the image of the dangerous appetizer. "Thank you!"

"For what?"

"For making me laugh."

"Thank me by dancing with me tonight."

"Sure." My steps felt lighter already.

Chapter 25

We saw the night part-timers off and made quick work of the start-of-day checklist. Mason and Joey were both dressed like Fred Astaire on a rehearsal day in tight T-shirts and pleated pants. They would be in tuxedos for tonight. They had never wavered in their belief in Buckingham's all week. I'd hugged both of them as Lady Anthea and I headed out. They bowed to her. The gesture had become a thing between the three of them. As hard as she tried, she couldn't keep herself from snickering every time.

"What should I say if anyone asks where you are?" Shelby called.

"Just say where we are."

At ten o'clock Lady Anthea and I were pulling up in front of Dayle's house. She opened the screen door and stuck her head out to look up and down the street. We heard classical music coming from the back of the house. "Get in," she whispered. "Were you tailed?" A colorful Hermès scarf covered her head, stylishly knotted at the back of her neck.

"Don't think so," I said.

"At least not by Mary Jane. We haven't called her yet," Lady Anthea said. "Since she lives so close we were afraid she would arrive before us."

We walked in, stepping carefully on the paper-covered floor and around industrial-sized paint cans. Dayle took another look out. "What do you mean? Who else might be following you?"

"Chief Turner is never far away," Lady Anthea said, giving me a look and a *don't argue* raised eyebrow.

"I'm sure there's an interesting story behind that," Dayle said. "And I'm betting it started Monday night at Gilligan's. How long did you stay anyway?"

The casual question threatened to unnerve me. When would I go back to a simple life that included late and lazy nights out with my friends?

"Wait," I said. "That night was one of the few times I stayed out later than you." She laughed in agreement. "You were gone before Chief Turner showed up, so why do you think anything—and I'm not saying it did—started then?"

"Barb and Red told me about how he was looking at you with those beagle eyes. By the way, where's your car?"

"Parked around the corner," I said.

"Oh, right. But won't she assume you two are here when you call to ask her to come over?"

"We didn't want her to know *she* is here," I said, pointing to Lady Anthea.

"We didn't want her to know *she* is here," Lady Anthea said at the same time, pointing at me.

We laughed and I said, "She doesn't like either of us right now. She knows Chief Turner's information on the value of the paintings came from her." I nodded in Lady Anthea's direction.

"She saw quite clearly that Sue was the reason her feminine tricks didn't work on the chief," Lady Anthea said, pointing right back at me.

"Can I call her from your land line?" I asked. "If her caller ID shows my name, she may not answer. Unless you want to do the honors?"

"I can't! I told you I'm a horrible liar!" Dayle said.

We followed her and Dottie into the kitchen, which was the neatest room we'd been through. She picked up a remote from the table and turned the music coming from the Bose radio off.

I dialed the number I'd written on my palm. After a generous number of rings, I was about to hang up when someone answered.

"Hello." I'd woken her up.

"Mary Jane?"

"Yes, who is this?"

"It's Sue Patrick." She groaned and I was afraid she was about to hang up. "I need your help."

She didn't respond, but I didn't hear a click either, so I figured I'd keep going. "I'm at Dayle Thomas's house. Do you know her? She's a photographer?"

"I've seen her work."

"Well, she's—uh—" I realized I hadn't asked Dayle if I could say anything about her having cancer. I looked over at her.

She bobbed her head up and down, smiling. She was all in and I kept going.

"I don't know if you're aware of this, but she has cancer. Chemo has been kicking her butt and she's having a rough morning. I was wondering if you would come over and see her since you're a nurse. And maybe you can tell her if you agree with the prescriptions she's taking?"

"I hear she's photographing people now, not just animals," she said, in mid-yawn. I imagined a wheel turning inside Mary Jane's head. She was being asked to help someone fighting cancer and she'd started working out how to turn the deed to her advantage. Not pretty. "Who's that at my door at this ungodly hour?" I heard bumps, bangs, and cursing as she made her way through her house.

"As if I don't get enough of that old fool every afternoon," she said under her breath, unaware someone with ears like a dog, namely me, was on the line. Then in a louder but distant voice, "Hold your horses." She brought the receiver back to her face. "Be there in half an hour."

"The front door will be unlocked. Just come in," I said, sticking to my script. I hung up and told Dayle and Lady Anthea what she'd said. Of course, leaving out the first part with her less than altruistic motive.

"That gives us just enough time for a cup of tea," Dayle said, pointing to the three china cups and saucers on the counter by the stove. "I have loose tea because I thought you would prefer it."

Lady Anthea clapped her hands. "I've reached civilization!"

Dayle laughed. "I made tea like this last night. It was really good. You brought something new to Lewes."

We sat around the table and waited for the water to boil.

"Don't watch it," I said. "You know how that goes. Speaking of watching, where should we hide before Mary Jane gets here?"

Dayle got up and spooned tea into three tiny mesh baskets. Then she poured water into the cups. "I think we can all fit in the closet under the stairs. That door's original and the slats are spaced about a quarter of an inch apart."

I wasn't wild about being crammed into a closet, but I would do it for the cause. I dreaded seeing the look on the face of my gentry-partner.

"Perfect," Lady Anthea said.

"You're being a good sport!" I said, surprised.

"I was referring to the tea."

"If we don't hide, we won't be able to see how familiar she is with the house in its current state, Dayle said. "She came through on the Lewes House Tour last year, but she shouldn't have been inside since."

"I'll be fine. Fristhden has many cubbyholes that my brother and I played in when I was a girl."

"Dayle, we hate to ask you to hide with us but we need to see how Dottie responds to her when she lets herself into the house," I added. "If Dottie is with you we won't be able to tell if Mary Jane is a stranger or not. Her reaction would probably be different."

Dayle took another sip of tea then went to stand in the doorway to the kitchen, facing the front of the house. "I was going to be the lookout for you, but how about if I close the front door? That way no one will be able to see us through the screen door, and you can stay in the kitchen until Mary Jane gets here." Suddenly she froze.

I had heard it too. Footsteps crunched up the gravel path to the house. I had been half expecting Mary Jane to get here late, not a few minutes early. Lady Anthea checked her watch.

Dayle went to the door.

"What are you doing here?" Dayle demanded in an annoyed voice. Without looking back at us, she swung her hand a few inches back, arm straight. *Stay*, the gesture said.

"I just want to talk. That's all," a male voice pleaded. I knew that voice. I had heard it recently.

My eyes met Lady Anthea's. She squinted in concentration, then her eyes flew open wide. She reached around to the nape of her neck and flicked her wrist. A ponytail?

"Rick Ziegler?" I mouthed.

"Not a good time!" Dayle said.

"It's never a good time any more, is it? You're shutting me out!"

"Just not now. If you leave, I promise we can talk later," Dayle said, calmer but insistent.

"When? Tell me when and I'll leave," Rick said.

"At the gala tonight," Dayle promised.

"I want two dances!"

The joy in his voice made me smile and Dayle laugh. "Two? You drive a hard bargain, Mr. Ziegler."

"Two *slow* dances or I go back to the street and yell how much I love you for all of Lewes to hear!"

"Okay, okay, two slow dances! Now leave and I'll see you in a few hours." Dayle closed the door and came back to us in the kitchen with a big grin on her face.

"My, my," Lady Anthea said.

"Uh-huh," I said. "I thought I knew all the latest Lewes gossip, but obviously, I don't. How long has this been going on?"

"Just before I was diagnosed. We got serious right away." She was back to standing in the kitchen door way. "Do you really think this Mary Jane Kerwin killed Henry?"

It was a blatant attempt to change the subject, but that was her right.

"I do," Lady Anthea said. "She's practically an art thief. She cheated her employer, who put trust in her, out of a substantial amount of money."

"I'm not as sure. I keep going back to the fact that, like you said, the two of them were cheating Peter Collins. What she does when she walks in here will tell us what we need to know," I said.

Lady Anthea looked at Dayle. "You were listening to Franz Liszt. Am I correct?" She pointed to the radio on the cabinet. I was grateful the question had been addressed to Dayle and not to me. "In his compositions, almost every musical phrase is the consequence of what came before it. Mary Jane learned Henry had a fiancée. Henry was murdered. I don't think that was a coincidence."

Dottie began barking.

"Shhh," Dayle said. "I hear someone. Quick, get in the closet."

Lady Anthea was mid-sip but put her cup down on table. We scrambled out to the hallway. Dayle was holding the door open for us and we stooped to get in without hitting our heads before she closed the door. "Be right there," she called down the hall, then she caught herself. "Oops," she whispered. She was supposed to be in the closet with us, and Mary Jane was supposed to let herself in.

"Go ahead," I whispered. "We'll just watch Dottie. That's good enough."

Dayle nodded and went to open the door. Lady Anthea and I watched through the slats of the closet door and immediately saw the limitation of our plan. Our vision was confined to three or four feet away down the hall. We wouldn't be able to see Mary Jane when she first came into the house. Hopefully, we'd be able to tell a lot by listening to Dottie since we couldn't see her either.

We heard the front door open.

"Hi—uhh." Dayle's voice had started on one note and then descended down the scale. "Can I help you?" Then louder, and clearly. "Chief Turner, isn't it?"

"That's right. Is Sue Patrick here?" I knew he wasn't one for the pleasantries, but that was abrupt even for him.

Silence from Dayle. I thought back about how scared she'd been after lying to the police the first time, and reached for the door knob. I would announce myself. Lady Anthea stopped my hand. She shook her head.

"She'll make quick work of him," she whispered.

Dayle shouldn't be put in that position. I would let this play out for another minute before I put a stop to it. I knew what I would say. I would close the door quickly behind me and tell him it was a bathroom.

"I haven't seen her," Dayle said.

Her voice was tentative, and I could imagine the suspicious look this would elicit from John.

"The Pet Place said she was here."

Pet Palace. I bit my tongue.

"Well, she's not. Bye."

"Wait," he said. "If you see her, tell her it's urgent that she call me."

"You'll see her at the gala tonight. You really should ask her to dance." Where the hell did come from?

"Ma'am, I don't think you understand. I need to reach her right away." Where Dayle had chattered, his voice was measured and weighty. "I've got to go."

The front door closed and Dayle came back to free us from our claustrophobia-inducing hideout.

I stretched my back and breathed in sweet liberty.

Chapter 26

"Where *is* Mary Jane?" Dayle asked in exasperation.

"I think we can assume she's not coming," Lady Anthea said on her way back to the kitchen.

"Peter Collins came to her door while we were talking," I said. "At least I'm assuming it was him since it was someone she sees every afternoon—"

"So she was just held up?" Dayle offered. "Can you stay a little longer? She should be here any minute."

I glanced over at Lady Anthea. "From what we've seen of her, I'm afraid it's more likely that she blew us off." I told them the part of my conversation with Mary Jane that I'd left out before. "Now, I'm wondering if when she said she would see us in half an hour, she was talking to him?"

"Dayle, is the kettle still on? I'd love another cup of tea," Lady Anthea said, making me wonder how hard life had been for her this week having to use tea bags. Was the tea at Buckingham's and at my house really all that bad?

When the refilled cup resulted in something between a sigh and a moan, I had my answer.

"Are you going to call Chief Turner?" she asked after the first sip.

"Nah, he can wait. When we leave here, let's go to the Best of the Past. If she's there, let's ask her why she didn't show."

"Good idea," Lady Anthea said. "If she's not there, it won't be a wasted trip, since I can get another look at the paintings."

Dayle jumped up. "I just thought of something. As much as I hate to see you go, there's a chance Peter Collins is still at Mary Jane's house. If he is, you can see the gallery without either of them being there."

"How would we get in if neither of them are there?" I asked. "There aren't any other employees who could let us in, are there?"

"He has seasonal help, but no one that would follow you around," she answered. "He keeps a spare key on the frame of the back door. Hurry!"

I looked at her closely. "Now you're acting and looking like your old self. Was it the tea tonic, our crazy scheme, or Rick's visit?"

She touched the side of her makeup-less face. "I've got so much to do. I'll see you tonight."

With a hug for Dayle and a goodbye pat on Dottie's head, we left and practically ran to the Jeep.

"What about Dayle and Rick Ziegler?" I asked.

"He's not my cup of tea," Lady Anthea said. "But he certainly is entertaining."

"He is that! Like when he gets drunk and blames it on that *one* evil beer found in every case."

"Sometimes opposites attract. Speaking of which, don't forget to call Chief Turner."

"I already did," I answered.

"When would you have called him?" she demanded.

"I meant, I already forgot to call him."

Chapter 27

The tourists had considerately left us a parking spot near the Best of the Past. The front door was propped open and the lights were on.

"It looks like we won't need to avail ourselves of the hidden key," Lady Anthea said as we walked in.

"I don't see anyone," I said, looking around.

"Well, someone is here," Lady Anthea said.

"If it's Peter Collins and he sees you, he'll be on you like a dog on a mailman's leg," I whispered, remembering how he'd fawned whenever he'd seen her. "Let's go." We were headed to the gallery section of the store when my cell phone rang. "Guess who this is," I said when I saw the name on the screen.

"Answer it this time!" she said. "Poor man."

I looked around and we were still alone, so I put the call on speaker and kept walking. The two large paintings were as beautiful and powerful as when we'd last seen them.

"Sue!" Chief Turner said.

I started parsing all I heard in his voice and couldn't name all the emotions in it. The tone said anger, but anxiety too.

"Where are you?" He sounded like he was running. Without waiting for my answer, he said, "Mary Jane Kerwin has been murdered. She tried to call 9-1-1, but her killer was already inside her home."

Suddenly the front door to the store closed, with enough force to rattle the glass, and when I heard the click of the lock, I knew who the killer was. Lady Anthea's eyes met mine.

Peter Collins stood in front of us, holding a gun. Though he was holding the ugly thing two-handed, his arms, hands, shoulders, and the gun shook. He pointed it first at me then at Lady Anthea.

"Sue," Lady Anthea said.

I took my eyes off the gun to look at her. She stood in front of the first of the Laliberte paintings.

"I've enjoyed every minute of this week. I wouldn't trade this time for all the country homes in England."

I smiled and hoped she could read my mind.

"Hang up," Collins hissed.

I stared at him a beat before remembering that I still held my phone.

Rather than end the call, I held the phone out to him. He looked at it, like he'd never seen such an apparatus before. Then his eyes darted back to us. To the left at me. To the right at Lady Anthea. He had a decision to make. Should he reach for the phone or not? The effort made the gun quiver, in fitful jerks.

"Hang up the call," he said finally.

I tapped the screen to do as he said.

"What are you doing?" he yelled at Lady Anthea.

She had backed up about two steps. I was only vaguely aware she'd moved because all I could see was the end of the barrel of that gun.

"Here's the phone," I said. I leaned over and with a flick of my wrist, sent the phone skidding along the floor.

His eyes tracked it for a few seconds before he brought his attention back to me. He blinked twice and took a deep breath, like there was a job ahead of him that he dreaded. Then he turned the gun on its side and moved it to his right hand. He was inspecting it. Was he looking for the safety? He slid a lever then went back to his two-handed grip. Damn, if I had known the safety was on, I could have run at him, but this was one in a long list of what I wish I had known when I needed to know it.

In my peripheral vision, I knew Lady Anthea had retreated another step farther back into the gallery. Was there a door in the back? I couldn't remember. How far behind us would it be? She could go for help.

"You knew what Henry and Mary Jane were up to all along, didn't you?" I asked as gently as I could.

Though I was looking straight at Peter Collins, I knew Lady Anthea was backing up again as I spoke. Right leg. Left leg.

She stopped when she reached the far end of the second painting. Now she was stock still. Maybe if I spoke again.

"They paid you chickenfeed for the first painting and then sold it to the highest bidder."

Lady Anthea had reached her arm up to the painting.

I went on, "They were about to do it again."

Collins's eyes darted to the painting that would have been sold off next, and I realized my misstep. He eyed the painting then Lady Anthea, who froze in place.

"If I had them arrested, I would have to admit I didn't know the true value of the artwork. I would have looked like a fool," he yelled. He thrust a step toward Lady Anthea with the force of his anger, jabbing the gun at the air between them like a saber.

"Those paintings had been in your family, hadn't they? For years?" My questions brought his attention back to me.

I heard metal clink to my left. Lady Anthea was doing something, but I didn't dare look to see what.

"I didn't know what to do!"

"Oh, but you did, Mr. Collins," I cooed. "On Monday you went to New York City to investigate, didn't you?"

He nodded causing his eyeglasses to slip down his nose a bit. Since he had gone back to holding the gun with both hands, there was little he could do about them.

When I stopped talking, Lady Anthea stopped whatever it was she was doing.

"You knew it was just a matter of time before the second painting went on the market," I suggested.

"Yes! A dealer in Greenwich Village who has known my family for years, and who is very familiar with our art collection, became suspicious when he saw the first sale and the listing for the second. That's who I went to see. He assured me the paintings were as valuable as my parents had told me they were! Henry and Mary Jane said no painting of a dog would ever be valuable to serious collectors." He stopped to take a breath. The gun lurched up again. "You see?" he yelled at me. Then he turned to Lady Anthea and demanded the same of her, "You see? I had to kill both of them."

When his eyes were off me, I stole a glance to see what she was doing. Her hand was practically behind the painting.

While I didn't know what the hell Lady Anthea was doing, I trusted her. I had to do my part. I had to start talking again.

"When you got back to Lewes you went to see Dayle, your friend, didn't you?" I asked. "On Monday night at Gilligan's she said you had tried to call her."

"Yes," he hissed. His eyeglasses were bothering him more and he tried to readjust them with the side of his hand. This only added to his agitation. "She wasn't home so I let myself in to wait. I heard a car pull up outside. I looked out the window and saw it was your van and Henry was bringing

Dottie in. I couldn't face him. I was afraid he would see by my expression how much I hated him and that I knew what he had done, so I hid in the kitchen. My intention was to leave her a note, but—" His voice trailed off.

"You saw Dayle's sleeping pills on the table?" I prompted him.

"I did, indeed, on my way out through her kitchen. Henry had left the door to the van open. I reached in over the driver's seat and dropped the pills into his water bottle. Then I came back here and waited to hear news of the driver of the Buckingham van being in a tragic accident." As Collins talked, he got a faraway look in his eyes, and the hand holding the gun drooped once more.

The thought that this was not exactly a surefire way to kill someone crossed my mind, but I had better sense than to be argumentative with someone holding me at gunpoint.

He transferred the weight of the gun from both hands, to hold it in his right and reached up to push his glasses back to the bridge of his nose. The simple move caused him to list to port, then he corrected and was listing to starboard. I watched as the pistol barrel swayed, rose, and fell with his every move.

He made a sound that was some combination of a wheeze and a high-pitched laugh. Then he was talking again, and the gun was back up level with my heart. "The dosage wasn't enough for someone his size. Instead of crashing the van, he came *here.* At first I thought he knew what I'd done and had followed me here to kill me." He shuddered at the thought, and the irony wasn't lost on me. I imagined myself back at Buckingham's, telling Shelby what he said, that is if I ever got back there. Then I heard a metal click from behind Lady Anthea.

"He had the audacity to let himself in the rear door of *my* gallery. That's how they treated me! I was afraid for my life until I remembered I had a steak knife in my desk drawer. Then I heard him call out for Mary Jane. He still thought I was away. I came out of my office and told him I heard a lot of noise coming from the back of van. He was stumbling around and still yelling for Mary Jane to help him. He kept saying he needed her."

His words conjured a mental image of my employee. That thought brought me full circle to Monday when I'd found the body and committed myself to finding out who had murdered him because I hadn't been there for him. I had listened to Collins's ranting, but I'd had enough and now I had to speak up for his victim. "I'll admit Henry was an unsatisfactory employee in just about every way possible, but he was part of the Buckingham Pet Palace crew." I narrowed my eyes and dared him to do his best.

Peter Collins was determined to make his point. "He didn't deserve your loyalty any more than Mary Jane Kerwin deserved mine. He didn't want to check on the dogs in that van. He said he didn't care about them. I, *I* had to convince him to go to the van." His voice was rising in volume and he was back to punctuating the words with juts in the air with the gun. "I climbed in behind him and then I stabbed him."

"Brilliant," a British accent whispered.

"Then I donned gloves to drive the van to Cape Henlopen Drive, and I walked back here."

"Sue!" Lady Anthea yelled and I turned to her. She shoved the end of one of the paintings my way and I grabbed it. It swung out from the wall. Then she unhinged the other end and lifted it higher. "He won't shoot the painting!"

Shielding ourselves and using the element of surprise, we charged him with the canvas, yelling at the top of our lungs. We had used his weakness, his love of possessions, against him. I couldn't see Peter Collins as we ran at him, but I heard him bellow in mental agony. That's when I heard someone banging on the glass of the front door. The door gave and seconds later we heard an "oomph." From beneath the painting, we saw Collins in a heap on the floor.

"Take it easy, ladies," said a now familiar baritone voice.

We lowered the artwork with its ornate frame. Thanks to the miracle of adrenaline, it had felt light, but it wasn't. John Turner took it from us and leaned it against the wall. Two uniformed Lewes police officers, one female and one male, pulled Collins from the floor and led him, ranting and spent, out of the Best of the Past.

Lady Anthea leaned against the wall next to the painting. She was fighting back tears with one breath and laughing with the next. I heard her say something about being happy that we were still on this side of the River Styx.

John had been watching me to check my emotional state, but I had no intention of breaking down in front of him. Now he looked at me for translation of what she'd said. No idea.

"Right now I'm happy to be, well, anywhere," I said and walked around him. There was a gala to get ready for.

Chapter 28

I stood in the receiving line next to Lady Anthea, Abby, Dana, Mason, Joey, and Shelby. The yellow orchids and coral roses in the pots glowed in the moonlight. Was it really just five days ago that I had chosen those?

The procession of Lewes citizens stalled regularly when a guest asked about our involvement in what Rick Ziegler had dubbed, "the gunfight at the O.K. Antiques Store." This time it was Betsy Rivard who wanted to hear how we'd outsmarted Peter Collins.

"Sue and I yelled like banshees," Lady Anthea said. "Which, as you know, is a Gaelic term referring to…" I intervened and got the line moving again.

Barb Moulinier, dressed in a floor-length, actually beach-length, white lace dress, made her way to the end of the buffet table and picked up the microphone. With one hand, she flicked it on, and with the other, she motioned for me to join her. The evening had begun with a welcome from me, and an introduction of Lady Anthea.

As the sun set, the guests ate their fill and then some. We'd enjoyed soup shooters, fried olives, and feasted at the raw bar. Wayne had wholeheartedly approved of the fare, particularly of the roast beef sliders with horseradish. The classical guitarist had started with "I Can't Help Falling in Love", and moved on to "Love Me Tender." The waitstaff kept everyone's glass filled with either Orange Crush, the state cocktail of Delaware, or with wine. Bartenders served craft beers on tap or in a bottle.

I left the Buckingham team and went to join Barb, and the guitarist joined us. "You clean up good, Ms. Patrick," he said. I wore a yellow silk mini-dress and canary-yellow diamond stud earrings that had been my mother's.

"You're looking mighty sharp yourself," I said. He wore a white tuxedo jacket over white bathing trunks, and a bow tie.

"Good evening," Barb said to the two hundred-plus guests. "We'll begin the entertainment part of this perfect night with a duet."

She and I both looked around for my singing partner. Chief Turner was walking toward the stage. I thought he was coming closer to hear better, so my mouth dropped open when he walked up to me. I stared in shock. As Lady Anthea would say, I was gobsmacked. "You?" I whispered.

"Don't look so surprised. I am a baritone, after all," he said, taking the microphone from Barb. He was still in uniform. I had asked him about that when he came through the receiving line, and he'd said that even though the two murders had been solved, seeing him in uniform would make citizens feel better. I didn't believe him for a second.

It wasn't the time nor place to go into Elvis singing two and a half octaves, yada yada, so I took a deep breath and waited for the guitarist to begin the opening chords of "Today, Tomorrow and Forever."

John started to sing the love song, looking into my eyes.

I sang when it was time for Ann-Margret's part.

To my surprise, we harmonized pretty well.

"None of the dogs howled so I guess we did okay," I said to him, over the applause and cheering.

Barb took the microphone and raised her hand to try to get order. No luck. Dana, Shelby, Mason, and Joey were jumping up and down, yelling, "Encore." Then the lights on the beach lit up forming a perfect square with our local disc jockey, Awd-E-O, all set up and ready to go.

"Let's dance!" Barb yelled to the crowd.

I was wearing white ballet slippers and I pulled them off and threw them under a table. Dogs and humans stampeded out as Awd-E-O started "C'mon Everybody." The whole Buckingham team ran to meet Abby and me in the center. My toes sunk into the sand, which was still warm from the day's sun.

Elvis sang, and we snapped out fingers.

Then I saw Lady Anthea was there, on the other side of Abby.

"You're not wearing shoes!" I yelled.

She laughed. "The sand feels utterly amazing."

When the song was over she, Abby and I walked to the side of the dance sand. "Lady Anthea, I need to ask you something. Were you serious about taking full-time responsibilities here? Do you want to stay?"

"I think I'd like that," she said, then she looked around at Rick and Dayle, dancing with a barking Dottie, at Charles Andrews and So-Long moving more sedately, at Dana, Mason, and Joey with more up-to-date moves. "Would I fit in?"

"This might be the Orange Crush talking, but do you think you could hold back on the talk about operas, Shakespeare, and mythology?"

"Is that what those drinks are called? I had three and this might be them answering, but I doubt it. How about if I limit them to one an hour?"

"Deal!"

John Turner was walking toward us, sans shoes, and the next song was starting.

"I know just who I want to dance with for this number!" I said.

He reached his arms out but he wasn't who I had in mind.

I leaned down and picked Abby up and sang "Hound Dog" to her.

He followed us to the dance floor sand and swayed and sang with us. "I hardly recognized you when I first saw you tonight," I yelled over the music.

"Why not? I'm still in uniform, except for my shoes. I have no idea where they are."

"It's everything. You look more relaxed than you've been all week."

"I haven't relaxed since Walton ran you off the road. I was more than worried about you. I hated the way that made me feel." He started to lean over to talk to me, but I was still holding Abby.

"I remember you storming off into the night. You didn't seem concerned for me."

"I wanted to stay there for you and I needed to do my job, both. Do you think you could put that dog down?"

"No," I said.

"I'll make you a deal. I'll give dogs a chance, if you give me one."

I put Abby down to go play with So-Long, Dottie, Robber, and Paris then I shook John's hand. "Deal," I said.

Meet the Author

Lane Stone is a native Atlantan. She, her husband, and their dog Abby live in Alexandria, VA during the week and in Lewes, DE on the weekend. When not writing, she enjoys characteristic baby boomer pursuits: hiking in various countries and playing golf. Her volunteer work includes conducting home visits for A Forever Home, a dog foster organization, and media/ communications for the Delaware River & Bay Lighthouse Foundation. She's on the Political Science Advisory Board of Georgia State University..

Printed in the United States
by Baker & Taylor Publisher Services